Why didn't he touch her? He was only inches away, and she could sense the tension tightening his body. Yet he only looked at her with those crystal eyes and . . . waited.

She couldn't stand it. She whirled and went into his arms, sliding her arms around his waist.

Louis stiffened. "Mariana?"

Warmth, strength, sleek, corded muscle against her softness. An erotic shock jolted her as she felt her body responding to his. "Just testing your hunting instinct."

His hands tangled in her hair. "My 'instincts' may give you more than you bargained for. All I could think of during dinner was—"

"That's what I wanted you to think about." Her voice shook slightly but she hoped he didn't notice. "That's what I planned on."

"Oh, yes," he said, a faint bitterness tinging his words. "How could I forget your plan?" He tilted her head back, his lips hovering over her mouth. "You have a wonderful neck, Mariana . . . and fantastic skin." His lips caressed the hollow where her pulse pounded crazily.

She gasped at the fire that raced through her, and he lifted his head. "Come on, I can't take any more of this. Let's go to my room."

Instead, she pulled him to the summerhouse, flung open the door, and ran inside. Darkness. Intimacy. The scent of roses. . . .

WHAT ARE *LOVESWEPT* ROMANCES?

They are stories of true romance and touching emotion. We believe those two very important ingredients are constants in our highly sensual and very believable stories in the *LOVESWEPT* line. Our goal is to give you, the reader, stories of consistently high quality that may sometimes make you laugh, sometimes make you cry, but are always fresh and creative and contain many delightful surprises within their pages.

Most romance fans read an enormous number of books. Those they truly love, they keep. Others may be traded with friends and soon forgotten. We hope that each *LOVESWEPT* romance will be a treasure—a "keeper." We will always try to publish

LOVE STORIES YOU'LL NEVER FORGET
BY AUTHORS YOU'LL ALWAYS REMEMBER

The Editors

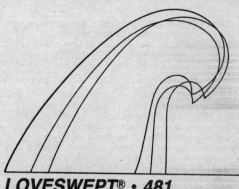

LOVESWEPT® • 481

Iris Johansen
A Tough Man to Tame

BANTAM BOOKS
NEW YORK • TORONTO • LONDON • SYDNEY • AUCKLAND

A TOUGH MAN TO TAME

A Bantam Book / July 1991

*If you would be interested in receiving protective vinyl
covers for your Loveswept books, please write to this address
for information:*

> Loveswept
> Bantam Books
> P.O. Box 985
> Hicksville, NY 11802

ISBN 0-553-44161-2

Published simultaneously in the United States and Canada

One

"Why Louis Benoit?" Gunner asked.

"It has to be Benoit," Mariana said. "I won't accept anyone else."

"Lord, you're stubborn." Gunner frowned. "It's not smart, Mariana. If you won't let one of our people handle the production end of your business, then let me go to Sheikh Ben Raschid and have him put it in the hands of one of his corporate executives."

"Which would be the same as using the Clanad." Mariana rose to her feet and moved restlessly to the casement window across the study. "I don't want Muggins, Inc. to be connected with either the Compound or Sedikhan. There have been too many rumors already."

"Which we've managed to squelch very efficiently," Gunner said. "Your argument doesn't hold water. There are ways we can control the flow of information, as long as we use our own people and are on home territory. Louis Benoit is an unknown quantity."

She glanced over her shoulder and wrinkled her nose at him. "How can you say that? You compiled a dossier on him that must be a foot thick."

"Well, half a foot perhaps." Gunner grinned. "And you said you wanted to know everything. Benoit has a checkered past. Didn't you find that his dossier made interesting reading?"

"Not really." She avoided his gaze and looked out at the charming bridge arching over the brook in the Chinese garden. "It was just curiosity. I actually knew what I had to know after reading about him in the *Wall Street Journal* and *Business Week*. He's a brilliant financial wizard who made his first million by the time he was twenty-five and became a billionaire by the time he was thirty. He's reputedly honest, doesn't mind taking chances, and is somewhat unorthodox in the way he runs his business. That's what I want for Muggins."

"He's also pure steel and tough as hell if you go against him. The man likes to be in control."

"Like you." She turned and smiled affectionately at him. "The pot calling the kettle black?"

"Maybe. But you know this particular pot is on your side."

"Benoit will be on my side too. He'd be a fool not to be, when I'm about to offer him the deal of the century."

"I don't like it. It's too damn dangerous." Gunner turned to the man sitting quietly in the easy chair in the corner. "She's your sister, dammit. Talk to her, Andrew."

"You've hardly let me get a word in edgewise."

Andrew's quizzical smile lit his fine features as he looked at her. "Why, Mariana?"

Mariana braced herself, carefully closing him out. She always had more difficulty with Andrew than Gunner—not only because of Andrew's strength but also because of the bond of affection between her and her brother. "I just told you why. I chose the man who would do the best job for me."

"No other reason?"

She met his gaze and sensed the probing gentleness, the loving concern. "What other reason could there be? I've never even met the man. You know I've never been out of Sedikhan."

"That's why I find it odd you didn't want to be surrounded by your own people on your first journey into the unknown."

She tried to smile jauntily. "Maybe I feel the need to try my wings."

"After burying your head in the sand all these years?" Andrew shook his head. "It's hardly logical that you'd want to kick up your heels and set out to conquer the world. You're afraid even to let me near you."

She immediately bristled. "I'm not afraid of you. Don't be ridiculous."

"Aren't you?" He stood up and strolled toward her. "Then let me—"

"The hell I will!" She glared at him, her hands clenching at her sides. "Back off, Andrew."

"Easy." He reached out and cupped her cheek in the hollow of his palm. "I'm not pushing you, little ostrich."

She relaxed and turned her head to lightly press

her lips to his palm. "Then stop worrying about me."

"It goes with the territory. You're the only sister I have. And I've told you before, you can't fight it forever, Mariana. It's a part of you and it could be more dangerous to repress than accept."

"There's nothing to repress." She laughed shakily as she backed away from him. "I'm not like the rest of you. I'm the cuckoo in the nest."

"The ostrich in the nest," Andrew corrected softly. "A frightened, lovable ostrich who doesn't realize that the fear is worse than the malady." He stepped forward and kissed her on the forehead. "If you get tired of hiding, you know I'll be here for you." He turned. "Let's go, Gunner. I'm sure Mariana has packing to do if she's leaving in the morning."

"That's it?" Gunner rose to his feet. "A great help you were."

"I'm just her brother." Andrew's blue eyes twinkled. "A brother's job is merely to support and comfort. You're the one who's supposed to protect and offer sound advice."

"Which everyone blithely ignores," Gunner said glumly. "You won't reconsider and stay in Sedikhan?"

Mariana shook her head.

"You're not making my job any easier." Gunner gazed at her a moment and then chuckled. "But what the hell. Easy is dull most of the time anyway. Maybe I need a little excitement to get my adrenaline flowing. Quenby says I'm getting stodgy."

"She's joking," Mariana said dryly. "After being married to you all these years she has to know if trouble doesn't come to you, you go out looking for it."

"Brat. No one understands what a peaceable man I am. Remember to call Quenby and say good-bye before you leave."

"I planned to stop by your house and Mom and Dad's tomorrow on my way to Marasef airport. I should arrive in Paris by ten in the morning and it will take me about an hour to get to Benoit's chateau. You've arranged to get me past the gates at Darceaubeau?"

Gunner nodded. "And, according to our information, Benoit spends most of the afternoon in the garden, so if you go directly there you won't have to deal with the servants. I've told our man to make sure you have a clear field from one until three tomorrow afternoon." He frowned. "But Benoit's got a damn good security team at the chateau. He's going to be suspicious as hell. Why the devil couldn't you just make an appointment at his office in Paris?"

"He wouldn't have seen me. When he comes back to France from New York it's usually because he's so exhausted he needs to be recharged. Darceaubeau is his sanctuary."

"Which won't make your intrusion any more welcome."

"I still prefer the chateau. I wanted the meeting to be informal. Business offices intimidate me."

"All the more reason for you to forget this nonsense and let us handle it." Gunner waved his hand as she started to speak. "Okay, okay, it's your project. I won't interfere as long as you call me every other night once you're inside the chateau."

His face hardened. "If you don't, you can expect hell to pay."

Andrew followed Gunner to the door but paused to look searchingly at her. His voice was soft as he asked the same question Gunner had, "Why Louis Benoit?"

He had obviously seen through her explanation. She started to speak, but thought better of it. She had always hated lies and evasions, and it was far worse to lie to the people you loved.

"No?" Andrew nodded understandingly. "Then all I can say is be careful. He's not a man you can program for your own convenience and, from what Gunner says, there's a good deal of volatility beneath his cool control."

"What are we going to do?" Gunner asked as soon as Andrew fell into step with him on the way to the car at the curb. "I don't like this one iota."

"You made that clear."

"Hell, she's only a baby. There's no way she can handle a man like Benoit."

"She's an adult and has a mind that Einstein would have envied."

"Dammit, you know what I mean."

Andrew knew exactly what he meant. Mariana was a mass of contradictions—blunt, loving, impulsive, with a bravado that never quite hid her sensitive vulnerability. "Perhaps you're being too protective."

Gunner gave him a narrowed look. "And you're being entirely too complacent. Why?"

"This may be good for her."

Gunner gazed at him, waiting.

"I've been worried about Mariana for the last year," Andrew said quietly.

Gunner stopped on the walk, paling. "Lord."

"Don't fall apart. It may not happen."

"And what if it does?" Gunner asked harshly. "We've got to keep her here where she's safe."

"Right now she may be safer out in the world."

"You can't be sure of that."

"No." Andrew felt a thrill of apprehension as he glanced back at the small house they had just left. They were taking a big chance letting Mariana go, particularly when he could sense something very strange in her attitude about this journey. Yet he had to trust the instinct that told him to let her leave them. "We can only hope I'm right."

Mariana watched the door close behind Gunner and Andrew and felt a twinge of panic. Andrew was right; Louis Benoit would never be malleable and she was probably crazy to insist on having her own way in this. She turned back to look out the window at the disciplined beauty of the Chinese garden. Everything in its place, peaceful, blessedly safe. Like her life in the Compound. Panic began to escalate within as she realized that tomorrow she was going to leave.

She could change her mind. She didn't have to leave the security she had cherished all her life and go out into the world. She could stay here and work in her laboratory and let Gunner and the council handle everything for her. Yes, she would run after Gunner and tell him—

"No!" She whirled away from the serene view of the garden and strode across the study and out into the hall. "Muggins!"

"Coming." Mrs. Muggins glided down the hall, her round blue eyes luminous, tight red curls shining in the fading light pouring through the foyer skylight. "It was good seeing dear Andrew again. He's looking well, isn't he?" She sighed. "I'm afraid the lad doesn't miss me at all now that he's wed. Oh, well, perhaps now I'll be able to concentrate on you."

"Have you finished my packing?"

"But of course, darlin'." A touch of indignation inflected Mrs. Muggins's Irish brogue. "Now you run along and take your shower and ready yourself for bed while I fix you a bite to eat."

"I'm not hungry."

"Just a bite won't hurt you." Mrs. Muggins turned and moved down the hall toward the kitchen. "Mr. Muggins is in the kitchen and I'll have him bring you a tray while I crate the batteries and extra parts. We wouldn't want to be caught short, now would we? How long will we be gone?"

"I have no idea."

"I suppose it doesn't matter. The trip will be good for you. I'm always telling you that you work too hard."

"Only lately," Mariana grumbled as she approached the curving staircase. "You know I can take care of myself. I can't figure out what's gone wrong with you."

"You're such a clever lass. I'm sure it will come to you soon . . ." Mrs. Muggins's voice faded away as she entered the kitchen.

Mariana swiftly climbed the stairs and entered her bedroom. Four pigskin suitcases were stacked neatly beside the door and her tailored terry-cloth robe was laid out on the bed. With her usual precise clockwork efficiency Mrs. Muggins would probably give her fifteen minutes to shower before Mr. Muggins arrived at the door with a tray.

She automatically started for the bathroom and then stopped halfway to her destination. What on earth was she doing? She had no intention of letting Mrs. Muggins dictate what she would or would not do, dammit. She didn't feel like taking a shower right now and had far too many things to do before her departure. She crossed to the desk, sat down, and opened the middle drawer. She would make a few lists of instructions to give to the council about the security she wanted arranged for her laboratory here in the—

Louis Benoit.

She gazed down at the cynical, jaded face of the man in the photograph in the drawer. The now-familiar tension gripped her. She had been lying to herself about the lists. It was this damn picture that had drawn her to the desk. She should never have taken the photo from Benoit's dossier. Ever since she had placed it in this drawer last week it had seemed to call to her, beckon her. Which was not surprising, she thought defensively. According to the dossier, Louis Benoit had been exerting a fascination over women for the majority of his thirty-six years. Crystal-gray eyes gazed warily up at her from a stunningly handsome face reflecting intelligence as well as Adonis-like good looks. This photo was only a head shot but the videotapes

Gunner had gathered showed Benoit to be tall and slim and able to move with the easy athletic grace of a male model. His good looks weren't the magnet drawing her, though. It was the indefinable sadness she sensed beneath his cynical facade. She reached out and gently touched the beautifully shaped lower lip of the man in the photograph. She inhaled sharply. The pad of her finger tingled as if she had touched flesh instead of glossy parchment. Sweet Mary, her imagination was becoming more uncontrolled with every passing moment. "Crazy," she whispered. "It's time it stopped, Louis."

The man in the picture stared up at her and, for a moment, it seemed the smile gentled, warmed, lost its disillusionment. Bonkers. Completely bonkers. She jerked her hand away from the picture and slammed the drawer shut. Thank God, she had set the machinery in motion to end this madness.

She jumped to her feet and strode toward the bathroom, snatching the robe from the bed as she passed. To the devil with showing the Mugginses they couldn't run her life. She felt terribly vulnerable and uncertain at the thought of confronting Louis Benoit tomorrow and needed all the soothing comfort she could get.

Not that she wouldn't be totally in control of the situation once she actually met the man. She had worked out the problem with her usual logic and precision, studying his needs, strengths, and idiosyncracies. She was now ready to resolve the dilemma she faced.

Dear heaven, she hoped she could resolve it. She couldn't go on this way.

The dream had to stop.

Louis's lids flew open, his muscles stiff with tension, his hands clenching with frustration at his sides.

"What's wrong?" Barbara murmured drowsily as she cuddled closer to him.

"Nothing. Only a dream."

"Like the one you had last night?"

"Yes." And the night before and the night before that and every night for the last four months.

"A nightmare?"

"Not exactly." Simply the mists and what lay beyond them, a feeling of aching loneliness, nagging incompletion, of searching and not finding. "Just a dream."

"Either it is or it isn't." She yawned. "I never dream."

"We all dream. You don't remember them, that's all."

"Maybe." She lost interest in the subject. "Well, now that you're awake . . ."

She thought he wanted her. It was true he always awoke from the dream aroused, though the dream wasn't sexual. Lord, Freud would have a field day with him. What was he worrying about? he wondered impatiently. He had come to Darceaubeau because he knew he had been working too hard and needed the break. Once his exhaustion vanished so would the dream.

Barbara touched him. She wanted to assuage

his lust with skill and the proper show of passion. He was always conscious of the core of coldness and self-interest motivating her every action. For an instant he felt a poignant sadness. Then he firmly dismissed it. Her coldness and his response to it had been the reason he had chosen to bring Barbara to Darceaubeau.

He was a realist and had long ago accepted this was how it had to be.

He was a realist, and dreams were for children.

He turned over and drew the woman into his arms. "How accommodating you are," he whispered.

Maybe this time his aching frustration would ease.

And perhaps the dream would stop.

"I have to talk to you."

Louis stiffened, startled as much by the belligerent tone as by the unfamiliar voice itself.

He turned and immediately relaxed as he saw the owner of the voice striding down the garden path toward him. Dark-haired, slim, petite, the girl looked no more than seventeen or eighteen and was dressed in jeans, tennis shoes, and a crisp white tailored cotton blouse. She must be one of the students that his gardener, Raoul, had hired to help, as he did every summer. "Are you speaking to me?"

The girl stopped before him, legs slightly astride. "My name is Mariana Sandell, Mr. Benoit. I have a business proposition for you." She gestured to a marble bench a few yards away. "You'd better sit down."

"Oh, had I?" He felt a mixture of amusement and annoyance. Everyone had a business proposition for him these days, but he hadn't expected to have his privacy invaded and be so boldly accosted by one of his own employees. Still, he had to respect the girl's initiative. "Your own nursery, I suppose?"

Her eyes widened in surprise. "Nursery? How did—" She broke off as she realized what he meant. "Oh, you mean flowers. You think I'm a gardener." She glanced around the rose garden and then wandered to the small pillared stone house a hundred yards away. "Actually, it's quite a nice garden. But it's a little flamboyant, and that summerhouse over there is almost as big as my home. I prefer more restraint, less showiness."

"Really? I would never have guessed it." Restraint was a term he wouldn't have associated with her. Wide-set brown eyes sparkled with zest and dark brown hair curled riotously about her heart-shaped face. In fact, her entire body exuded a restless vitality so strong it was like being near a lightning bolt. "I take it you're not one of Raoul's helpers?"

"Raoul?"

"My gardener."

She shook her head. "Maybe I shouldn't have dressed like this. I wanted to be comfortable on the plane and I came here straight from DeGaulle Airport, not bothering to change." She frowned. "You seem to be getting the wrong impression, and that's what I wanted to avoid. I know my size isn't very impressive and I probably look about twelve but there was no sense in wearing a tailored business suit and toting a briefcase. You needed to know that what you saw was what you'd get."

"What I'd get?" His lips twitched as he saw the color rise in the girl's cheeks. Lord, what magnificent skin. The velvet texture glowed gold in the afternoon sunlight and he had a sudden impulse to reach out and touch her cheek, feel the warmth beneath his fingertips. To his surprise he felt a stirring in his loins. Lord, he must be getting jaded if a child could arouse him. "Perhaps you'd better explain."

"I put that all wrong, didn't I? I'm not good with words." She lifted her chin. "But it wasn't that far off the mark this time. It's only fair to be as honest with you as possible."

The movement revealed the exquisite line of her throat; he could see her pulse pounding rapidly, erratically in the smooth hollow. The knowledge that she was nervous gave him a sense of primitive power curiously like that of a hunter stalking prey. "If you don't work for me, how did you get past the gates?"

"I have a friend who took care of it."

His gaze flew from her throat to her face. "I find that hard to believe. Even the most ingenious of the paparazzi hasn't found a way around my security system."

"My friend is very—" She broke off as she saw the grimness of his expression. "Don't blame your people. It's not their fault that—" She stopped again and asked with exasperation, "What difference does it make? I'm here now and I'm not trying to assassinate you or get a story for a scandal sheet. All I want to do is make you rich."

"I'm already rich."

"Richer."

"Do you think I'm so greedy?"

She shook her head. "But since you grew up in poverty, I can understand it's difficult to know how much is enough."

His gaze narrowed on her face. "You seem to know a great deal about me."

"It's only practical to research a potential business partner."

He gazed at her incredulously. "I never take partners."

"You will this time. I'm offering too much for you to refuse me."

He wondered why he was talking to this child when he should go back to the house and check to see what the hell had happened to gate security. Then he felt the hardening in his groin and realized with self-disgust exactly why he was still there. "You haven't offered me anything at all . . . yet."

"I was going to and then you got all bent out of shape because I breached your security."

"I'd say I have cause."

"I'm not offering you a nitpicking partnership in a fledgling nursery. I've got something that's going to rock the world."

He raised a distinctly skeptical brow.

"I *do*." She clenched her hands at her sides. "Look, I'm not a kid. I'm twenty-four years old." She took a deep breath and then blurted out, "And I'm a bloody genius, dammit."

Not a child; twenty-four—a woman. His attraction was all right then. It could happen. The knowledge brought a mindless surge of lust that he tried to suppress. What the devil was wrong with him? The reaction was too strong, too uncontrolled, and he had to maintain control at all costs. "How nice for you."

"You don't believe me. Oh, what the hell." She raised her voice and called, "Muggins!"

"Coming, darlin'."

Louis turned at the melodious voice and then stiffened in surprise as he watched Mrs. Muggins glide down the path toward him. "Good God, it's a robot!"

Two

At last Benoit's indulgent amusement had been replaced by shock, Mariana realized with relief. She should have had Mrs. Muggins with her in the first place.

"This is Muggins, Mr. Benoit. Actually, it's Mrs. Muggins."

Mrs. Muggins rolled forward and stopped before him. "And glad it is I am to be meeting you at last," she crooned. "Miss Mariana tells me you're going to be a part of our little family."

"I am?" Louis murmured. His gaze ran over her five feet of stainless-steel, rounded body that, in some bewildering fashion, managed to appear motherly. He stared at her amazingly lifelike sculpted features. Even the round blue eyes seemed to flicker with expression. "How . . . interesting."

"Go wait on the terrace, Muggins." Mariana strode to the bench and plopped down. "I'm sure Mr. Benoit will want to see you later."

"Louis," he corrected, still staring at the robot. "And I'm sure you're right. Fascinating . . ."

Mrs. Muggins turned and glided back toward the chateau, humming "Galway Bay" in a soft undertone.

"Exceptionally lifelike for metal," Louis said. "Batteries?"

"And a complex circuitry that took me ten years to develop." She frowned, her puzzled gaze following Mrs. Muggins. "I didn't think she'd leave so meekly."

Louis's brows lifted. "Ten years? That would have made you fourteen when you started."

"I told you I was a genius," she said simply.

"So you did." He stared at Mariana, then at the retreating back of Mrs. Muggins. "A pretty Star Wars demonstration, but there's no market for Robby the Robot. Not only does the public distrust robots, but also their uses are limited—and they're far too expensive to manufacture."

"Mrs. Muggins is no Robby the Robot. She's programmed to be the perfect housekeeper and nanny. And the reason robots' uses have been limited in the past was their decision-making capability. I've overcome that problem." She grimaced. "In fact, sometimes I think Mrs. Muggins is a little too decisive." She continued briskly, "And as for the cost factor, I've brought it down to the approximate price of a compact car. I don't consider that unreasonable, given that Mrs. Muggins and her friends will last fifty years with proper maintenance."

"Not unreasonable at all, if what you say is true."

"It's true. I could have marketed Mrs. Muggins

three years ago at twice that figure but now I've streamlined the—"

"Why did you come to me?"

"Why not? I need someone to set up production and handle distribution and marketing and so forth. Ten percent of the gross? Interested?"

"Let's say I'm intrigued." He met her gaze. "And wondering if you're a gift from heaven or a con artist trying to take me to the cleaners."

"Do you want me to wait while you make up your mind?" She grinned. "It shouldn't take long. You always make quick decisions."

"Do I? How do you know?" He nodded. "Ah, I remember. Research."

"Yes." Dear heavens, he was stunning. She had told herself the reality could never be as strong as the image she had held of him, but she had been wrong. The casual navy-blue cords and dark gray sweater he wore were lent elegance by the slim grace of his body. The strong sunlight lit the classic contours of his face and revealed the blue lights in his black hair and every line of his wonderful mouth . . . She pulled her gaze away from his face. "Research."

"How do you know I won't try to cheat you and steal your ideas?" His voice was deeper than she had imagined, his words almost free from accent except for an occasional Gallic intonation.

"Mrs. Muggins is patented and the council has drawn up contracts to protect my interests."

"Council?" He strolled over and sat down on the bench beside her.

"Legal counsel," she said quickly. "Naturally, I

have legal representation. I had them draw up the contracts for you to go over."

"I'm glad you have someone to protect your interests."

He was inches away, not touching her, but she was acutely conscious of the warmth his body was emitting, the lemony scent of soap and after-shave. She started to tremble. Sweet Mary, don't let him notice his effect on her. "And you would never steal from me anyway."

"I'm touched by your trust."

His tone was mocking again, and she felt a swift jab of pain. How foolish to feel so hurt when it didn't really matter what he thought of her. It was only necessary that he provide her with what she needed, and then they could both go their own ways. "It's not a matter of trust when one evaluates the character of a business acquaintance and makes judgments. You do it every day."

"Granted."

"But you're denying my ability to do the same thing." Her brow wrinkled with concentration. "And it's not because I'm a woman. According to your dossier, you have great respect for women in the business world. It must be me personally. I've put you on the defensive."

He frowned. "Ridiculous."

"No." She smiled. "It's what I wanted to accomplish but I was afraid I'd blown it. Wariness on your part is definitely needed in our relationship." She jumped up and reached out and pulled him to his feet. "Come on, we'll go back to the house and—" She shouldn't have touched him, she thought desperately. It was a mistake. The flesh of her hand tingled where it grasped his and yet she couldn't seem to let go. Her heart was pounding so hard he must be able to hear it.

He *did* know. His stare was fixed on the betraying pulse point in the hollow of her throat. She quickly released his hand and stepped back. "I'll have Mrs. Muggins give you a demonstration, then we'll examine the blueprints and spec sheets and you can call your lawyers to go over the contracts and then—"

She stopped, braced herself, and then said in a rush. "But you'll have to send her away."

He stiffened. "Who?"

"Barbara Cambrel."

"Is there anything you don't know about me, dammit?"

She smiled tremulously. "Not much. Send her back to New York."

His gaze narrowed on her face. "And why should I do that?"

"We're going to be very busy for the next few days and we don't want any information leaked by curious outsiders."

"Barbara isn't curious about my business affairs."

"But she's very mercenary and Muggins, Inc. will eventually be worth billions." She stared at him wonderingly. "Why are you arguing about this? She doesn't mean anything to you. At times, you even dislike her."

"I believe I'm becoming a little annoyed with what you believe is indepth knowledge about me. How the hell do you think you can know what I feel for someone?"

"Sorry. I'm probably handling this all wrong." He was still frowning, and she finally blurted out the truth. "I'd much rather forget all this *folderol* and go back to my laboratory. I'm not accustomed to this kind of thing and it frightens me."

His expression softened. "No one would ever guess," he said dryly. "You undermine my security, barge into my garden, and tell me to send away my mist—"

"You won't miss her," Mariana promised. "We'll be too busy."

His gaze wandered back to the hollow of her throat before lifting to her face. Then a faint smile touched his lips. "Do you know? I imagine you're right."

"And you'll send her away as soon as we get back to the chateau?"

He looked away from her as he began to stroll down the path toward the chateau. "Yes, I'll send Barbara away."

"Well?" Mariana watched Louis push away the contracts and specs on the desk in front of him. "You're satisfied?"

He leaned back in the executive chair. "Remarkable." He studied her. "You just may be the genius you say you are. I'm no engineer, but I've read enough blueprints to realize that this could revolutionize robotics."

"And make you another fortune." Mariana grinned. "You'll call your lawyers?"

He nodded. "I'd be a fool not to want in on the ground floor. It should prove an interesting project." He paused. "However, there are a few points in the contract we may have to negotiate. Your total approval of the programming of the robots isn't reasonable considering—"

"That's not negotiable," she said flatly. "I'm not building assembly-line robots. A good deal of their value will lie in the personal quirks and personalities programmed into each individual unit. My Mugginses are going to be created to live and work harmoniously with the people who own them and I want their programming to reflect sweet individuality."

"And does Mrs. Muggins have as agreeable a personality as you want?"

"Well, I still have a *few* kinks to iron out . . ."

"And it states here you're to be solely responsible for security." He shook his head. "No deal. You have no idea the violence and industrial espionage a project like this could generate. I want my own people on it."

"I got past your security people today."

"Which means there will be new people at that gate tomorrow."

"You're not going to fire them? Please, don't. It wasn't their fault. I told you—" She jumped to her feet. "We'll talk about it tomorrow."

"Just a minute. There are several other clauses with which I can't agree. I'll want twenty-five percent of the gross and I won't be a figurehead in any project. I'll want full control of the distribution process and—"

"Call your attorneys while I unpack and settle in. Do you care which bedroom I take?"

He went still. "You're staying here?"

"Of course. It will be much more convenient for both of us." She moved toward the door. "While I unpack I'll have Mrs. Muggins prepare dinner for us. I don't want to impose on your staff—especially not on your chef. You prefer French cuisine?"

"I have a choice?"

She glanced over her shoulder in surprise. "Naturally. I made her an expert cook in Chinese, Mexican, East Indian, Greek, Ital—"

"French cuisine will be fine."

She nodded. "If you change your mind just tell Mrs. Muggins. The cuisine is irrelevant to me. I'll meet you in the dining room at eight."

She left the study and moved quickly down the hall toward the staircase. Now to unpack her suitcase and call Gunner to tell him everything was proceeding according to her plans and he needn't worry.

It was true. There was absolutely nothing to be nervous about. Louis had agreed to take on the project. The first business steps had been taken and now she just had to get on with it. And, most importantly, she knew he'd been aware of her physically for at least a few moments in the garden!

Merciful heavens, she wished she could stop shaking.

"I didn't know we were dressing for dinner." Louis's gaze slowly ran over her as she came down the stairs; his eyes lingered on the upper curves of her breasts, bared by the low neckline of the cocktail-length gown. "Quite a change. Is this your alter ego?"

"No." She lightly touched the orange taffeta of the skirt of her gown with a caressing hand. "I like wonderful textures and I don't get a chance to dress for dinner very often at home. We live casually."

"And where is home?"

"The Compound." She moved down the hall toward the dining room and quickly changed the subject. "Did you get hold of your lawyers?"

He fell into step with her. "They'll arrive tomorrow afternoon. Would you like to call your legal people so they can attend?"

"No, they've done their part. The contracts stand as is or it's no deal."

His jaw squared. "Then it may be no deal. I'm not going to be dictated to, Mariana."

"We'll see." She glanced sidewise at him. "By the way, I sent the servants away for the next few days. I told them you wanted to test Mrs. Muggins's capabilities. I hope you don't mind?"

"Would it do me any good if I did?" His lips twisted. "You seem to be taking over."

"Only for the next few days." She entered the dining room and glanced around approvingly. Candlelight, creamy damask cloth, pink roses arranged in a crystal bowl. Mrs. Muggins had done very well. "Hmmm . . . a week, I'd say. Then I won't bother you anymore."

"Won't you?" He seated her in her chair and moved to his place across the table. "Puzzles always bother me. Compound? It sounds like a military fort."

"No, it's a sort of town . . ."

"In the United States?"

She gazed at him warily. "No, why did you think I was American?"

"Your accent. Surely your information on me didn't neglect the fact I've lived primarily in the U.S. for the last fifteen years."

"My mother is American, but the Compound isn't in the United States."

"Here in France?"

"No."

"What nationality is your father?"

He was asking too many awkward questions. She quickly picked up her wineglass and changed the subject. "I lied, you know."

His gaze narrowed on her face. "About what?"

"The gown. I wore it because I knew you liked the color." She didn't look at him as she took a sip of wine. "You like yellow and burgundy, but you're particularly fond of this shade of tangerine."

"Oh, am I?" He leaned back in his chair. "And why should you want to please me?"

She took another sip of wine. "The usual reason." She looked up to meet his gaze. "I want to go to bed with you tonight."

A muscle twitched in his cheek, but his expression remained impassive. "I'm flattered you consider me so irresistible."

She ignored the sarcasm in his tone and kept her tone carefully cool. "You must know you're an attractive man, but that's not the reason I want to go to bed with you. I believe we need to cement the agreement and this seems to be as good a way as any."

"A handshake is inadequate?"

"It's been my experience that men find it a bit more difficult to cheat a woman they've slept with. And you're proving more difficult than I thought in regard to those contracts. Tomorrow your lawyers come and you may give me much less trouble if you have a pleasant memory or two." She smiled. "Besides, I've deprived you of your mistress. It's only proper that I give you a suitable replacement."

"Very logical."

She nodded. "I'm always logical."

"And calculating."

"I couldn't have built Muggins without that kind of mentality." She took another sip of wine, her hopes plummeting. Why had she thought she could pull this off? She was overdoing it and coming off as an unappetizing woman, perhaps even a mercenary bitch. Judging by his expression Louis was going to throw her out on her ear at any moment. "Of course, I'm probably not as alluring as your Barbara, but I'm not ugly, and I'm willing to do anything you ask of me."

"Anything?"

"Without exception." She smiled at him from across the table. "I want to make you happy. Muggins, Inc. is very important to me."

"It must be."

"You sound so grim. Why? We both know sex is always either a commodity or a game."

For an instant his expression was infinitely weary. Then he smiled sardonically. "My apologies. You took me by surprise. You're a little young to be so cynical."

"I learned a long time ago that a businesswoman

has to use every weapon she has in order to gain the advantage."

"And sex is a weapon?"

"One of the most powerful in the arsenal."

"I see." He lifted his own glass to his lips and looked at her over the rim. "You're wrong, you know. I do find you alluring. I've wanted you since the moment I saw you."

Her heart gave a leap and she had to quickly school her expression. "I'm surprised. I thought you believed I was—"

"A child? I did. It didn't make any difference. Though I was a little worried I was turning into an aging *roué* about to prey on a teenager." His gaze was frankly sensual as it drifted over her throat, down to her low neckline. "How pleasant to know I needn't have worried after all. I'm sure if any preying is done it will be you who does it."

"I admit I've always been aggressive about getting what I want."

"I look forward to testing the truth of that statement. I do have to warn you, I have no intention of letting my business decisions be swayed by anything personal between us."

"I'll take my chances." She tried to smile confidently. "I've found sometimes the effect is subliminal."

"We shall see. Your offer is very interesting. I don't believe I've ever had a woman give me such *carte blanche* with her person." His hand tightened on the stem of the glass. "What if I told you I wanted you to take off that gown and everything you have underneath it and dine with me *au naturel*?"

She could feel the heat rise to her cheeks and hoped the candlelight hid the color from him. She shrugged. "If you like. You'll have to help me with the zipper." She set her glass down. "But we'd probably end up not eating the great dinner Muggins has made for you. Wouldn't you prefer to wait until coffee?"

He gazed at her blankly and then threw back his head and started to laugh. "By all means, let's wait for coffee." He lifted his glass in a half-toast. "I've always preferred to anticipate my pleasures. We'll have a nice, leisurely meal, during which I'll look at you and imagine everything I'm going to do to you." His voice lowered to sensual softness. "Anything?"

"Of course. I said so, didn't I?" she said briskly. "I'm at your disposal."

"Here we are." Mrs. Muggins glided through the doorway leading to the kitchen carrying a tray bearing rolls and a clear soup. "It's a grand meal I've fixed. You both must eat heartily now."

"You didn't eat more than a few bites." Louis lifted his coffee cup to his lips. "Mrs. Muggins definitely disapproved."

"Mrs. Muggins always disapproves. It's part of her nanny programming. I wasn't hungry." The strain of maintaining this cold and brittle facade during dinner had stretched her nerves to the breaking point. She couldn't have forced down another bite and was having trouble keeping her hand from trembling as she held the coffee cup. "Did you enjoy the meal?"

"Excellent." He smiled. "Though I didn't taste much. I found myself oddly absentminded."

She felt the heat rise to her cheeks. He had sat there perfectly at ease, making polite conversation, and all the while he had made sure she knew exactly what he had been thinking. A lift of the eyebrow, the possessiveness of his gaze on her breasts and shoulders, an occasional sensual smile. She had always thought gray eyes were icy, but there was nothing the least bit cool about the way he had regarded her. Her cup clattered as she abruptly set it back on the saucer. "I'm tired of this. Are you ready?"

He gazed at her in mock surprise. "Are you speaking of my physical state?"

"No." She pushed back her chair and got to her feet. "I told you I wasn't good with words, and that includes double entendres. I'm going for a walk in the garden. Coming?"

"Don't you ever sit still? You remind me of a firecracker, or a candle lit at both ends."

She stopped in the midst of turning away from the table, her gaze flying to his face. "A candle?"

"Did I say something wrong?"

"No, you only reminded me of a poem I read once."

"What poem?"

Her voice was only a breath of sound as she quoted.

My candle burns at both ends; It will not last the night;

But ah, my foes, and oh, my friends—it gives a lovely light!"

"Edna St. Vincent Millay, isn't it? You must be fond of her work if you remember it that well."

"It just stuck." She tried to shrug carelessly. "Most of her stuff is too depressing for me." She moved toward the French doors. "Coming?"

"I wouldn't miss it." He stood up and threw his napkin on the table. "Do you need a coat?"

"Not if Mrs. Muggins doesn't catch me," she muttered.

He chuckled. "You sound like a naughty little girl."

That had been a mistake. Little girls were vulnerable and appealing and he mustn't think her either of those things. She opened the French doors and moved out onto the terrace. "Is that the role you want me to play? Is that what turns you on?"

His smile faded. "That's not what I meant."

She moved to the stone balustrade and looked out over the garden. "Why do you spend so much time in the garden when you're at Darceaubeau?"

"How do you know—" He shrugged. "You have me at a disadvantage. It's not at all fair that you know so much about me when I know next to nothing about you."

"Why?" she persisted.

"It . . . The garden quiets me."

She turned to look at him. "And do you need quieting?"

"Don't we all? I grew up on the streets of Paris, and even after I was an adult it was many years before I could afford a house in the country." He half-leaned against the balustrade. "After dealing with the chicanery and power tactics of the boardroom it's a relief to come here where there's only natural growth and peace. I need it."

"Yet no one is better at power tactics than you."

"We all have a bit of the savage hunter in us. That's my Mr. Hyde persona." He smiled. "You should understand. You obviously have the hunting instinct too."

"Yes." She moistened her lips. "I suppose that's true."

Why didn't he touch her? He was only inches away and she could sense the tension tightening his body and yet he only looked at her with those crystal eyes and . . . waited.

She couldn't *stand* it. She whirled and went into his arms, sliding her arms about his waist.

He stiffened. "Mariana?"

Warmth, strength, sleek corded muscle hardening against her softness. An erotic shock jolted through her. She felt her breasts swelling, nipples hardening, pushing against the silky texture of her clothing. She burrowed her head in his shoulder. "Just testing the hunting instinct."

"Yours or mine?"

She was afraid her voice would tremble if she answered, so she remained silent.

"I guess it doesn't matter," he muttered. His hands tangled in her hair. "But my 'instincts' may give you more than you've bargained for. All I could think of during dinner was—"

"That's what I wanted you to think about." Her voice did shake but it was muffled against his chest, so perhaps he hadn't noticed. "That's what I planned on."

"Oh yes, your master plan." A faint bitterness

tinged his words. He tilted her head back. "How could I forget it?" He bent forward and his lips hovered over her mouth, then wandered downward. "God, you have a wonderful neck. It was one of the first things I noticed . . . fantastic skin and that lovely line . . ." His tongue darted out, caressing the hollow, where her pulse pounded crazily.

She inhaled sharply but it did little good—she still couldn't breathe. Heat was engulfing her, smothering her, and her knees were shaking so badly she would have fallen if she hadn't been holding on to him. She had told him she was aggressive and she knew it was out of character for her merely to stand there, but she couldn't seem to move.

He didn't notice. He was pulling the gown down, baring her breasts.

Cool air touched her nipples and she inhaled sharply.

He looked down at her, and she saw a muscle jerk in his left cheek. "Lord, what the hell is happening? I feel like a kid hot for—" He released her, stepped back, and grabbed her wrist, pulling her toward the house. "Come on. I can't take any more. It's time we got down to business."

Business. It was unreasonable to feel hurt at the cold term when this was exactly what she had wanted him to think. "Where are we going?"

"My bedroom. Where else?"

The room where he had probably made love to Barbara Cambrel last night and the night before. She hadn't guessed she would experience this wild feeling of rejection at the thought of him with another woman. She should be sensible and accept—

To hell with being sensible. "Not there." She tore away from him and ran toward the steps leading to the garden. "I don't want to go to your room."

"Where the devil are you going?"

"The summerhouse." She kicked off her high heels and ran down the steps. "Come on."

She heard him mutter something beneath his breath and then the sound of his footsteps pounding after her as she dashed down the path toward the stone house in the middle of the rose garden. "You're crazy. Dammit, it's only one room and there's nothing but a couch . . ."

She reached the summerhouse, flung open the door, and ran inside.

Darkness. Intimacy. The scent of roses.

Moonlight streaming through the glass pane of a long window facing north.

Louis was immediately behind her. He shut the door, enclosing them in still greater intimacy. "You're nothing if not unpredictable."

She turned around. "Unzip me."

"I can barely see . . ." His hands fumbled at the zipper and a hot shiver went through her as she felt the warmth of his knuckles on the flesh of her back. "Just a minute and I'll turn on the lamp."

"No!" The word had come too sharply and she quickly tempered her tone. "I like the darkness." It was a lie; she hated the dark. "It's softer." And unrevealing. He mustn't see her face during this part of it.

"That's more than I am. I've got it." The zipper slid down with a sibilant hiss and she felt the cool air on her bare back and then his hands as they slid around her rib cage and began to slowly rub her belly. "Lord, I want to *see* you."

"Later." Her stomach muscles clenched beneath his stroking and a tingling ignited between her thighs. She stepped away from him and the gown slipped over her hips and fell to the floor, followed by the petticoat. "Undress."

"Whatever you say." The mocking tone couldn't disguise the thickness of his voice as he pulled the sweater over his head. "The couch is to the left of the window. Make yourself comfortable, relax. It may be your last chance tonight. I don't think I'm going to be satisfied with only one time."

"Hurry." She took off her panty hose before moving quickly across the room toward the shadowy shape of a large couch. The pile carpet sank beneath her feet. The velvet texture of the cushions rubbed against her bare skin as she dropped down on the couch. It felt odd sitting naked in the darkness waiting for him to come to her. Since she could see little, her other senses heightened to exquisite sensitivity of the sensuous softness of the velvet touching her, the heady scent of roses, the sound of Louis's breathing.

She curled up in one corner of the wide couch, every muscle tight, her eyes straining to see him in the darkness. It was impossible. Louis was only a shadow and the moonlight streaming through the window revealed only an occasional silvery glimmer of light on his dark hair and the paler shadow of flesh as he quickly shed his clothing.

Then the shadow was moving toward her in the darkness.

A thrill of apprehension shot through her. She was no longer aware of her surroundings but of the softness of her flesh, the vulnerability of her small body.

"Damn this darkness," he muttered as he stopped beside the couch. "I want . . ." He reached out and touched her bare shoulder.

She gasped as sensation tingled through her.

He went rigid. "Lord, I've never had . . ." His hand moved down and cupped her breast. His breathing was becoming heavy, labored in the darkness. "Lie down . . ."

She scooted down as he fell to his knees beside the couch, his right hand opening and closing rhythmically on her breast while his other hand slid slowly down her abdomen and began petting the tight curls surrounding her womanhood. The action was so intimate, so erotic, it sent a shock through her. She made a low sound deep in her throat as his fingers tangled, pulled gently, teasingly.

"You like this?" His hand wandered down farther, searched and found. "And this?" He began plucking gently.

Her back arched off the couch. "Louis!"

"I see you do."

A long finger gently entered her. Another shock.

"So tight . . ." he whispered. "Lord, you're going to feel fantastic."

Another finger joined the first and began to slowly move in and out. She was so *full* and yet the motion was bringing a sensation of aching emptiness and unbearable tension. "This was what I was thinking about all through dinner. How I'd like to kneel before your chair and push up your skirt. I wanted to put my hands on you, to feel how warm and tight and—"

He broke off as she gave a moan, her need mounting to near-fever pitch.

"That's right, let me hear you." His voice was fierce as a third finger joined the others and began a rotating jerky motion. "I need to know you want me. Do you?"

Her teeth sank into her lower lip as a wave of heat moved over her. "Yes," she whispered. "Oh, yes."

"Are you ready for me?"

She bit her lips to keep back a cry as his fingers probed deeper. "Yes."

His hands left her and he was suddenly over her, between her thighs, his manhood nudging at the heart of her. "I can't wait any longer." His palms stroked her lower belly. "I need to be *here*. I want to fill you until there's no more to fill. I want to—"

He plunged deep within her!

This time she wasn't able to keep back the cry, but it didn't matter. He had to know now anyway.

"*Sacre bleu!* What the—"

"It's all right." Her hands quickly grasped his hips. "Don't worry about it." He was still frozen above her, deep inside her. "Go on."

"The hell I won't worry about it," he muttered. "But not now." He began to move. "Lord help me, I can't think of anything but this."

Darkness. Roses. Heat.

Burning. Stroking. Filling.

Her head thrashed back and forth on the velvet

cushions as she felt the tension spiraling, winding to unbearable tightness.

The sound of her own soft cries in the darkness.

The harshness of Louis's breathing. His voice muttering in French.

His movements were growing wilder, deeper, hotter. His hands slid around to cup her buttocks and he began to lift her to every thrust.

Vaguely, through her own physical and emotional turmoil, she sensed a change in him. His voice turned guttural, his thrusts more powerful; he was moving her as if she were a toy, making her take more of him. She was suddenly conscious of the strength of his body and her own helplessness against that strength.

"Louis?"

For an instant she didn't think he heard her. It was as if he were deaf, blind, mindless to everything but his own need. Then he stopped and she could feel the shudder that went through him. "Don't worry," he said thickly. "It's all right now." He began to move again, a rhythm too wild to be described as gentle but lacking that mindless animalistic drive.

She couldn't breathe.

She was burning.

No, melting.

Louis gasped. "*Maintenant, ma petite* . . . It has to be . . ."

Maintenant . . . Now! The tension exploded, shattered.

She dimly heard Louis cry out. He went rigid and then collapsed on top of her.

Was it done? Mariana wondered hazily. The

tension had been replaced by a delicious languor, but it didn't feel finished. In some mysterious fashion it seemed as if something had been started that should go on forever, that *would* go on forever. . . .

But Louis was moving off her and standing up. "Stay there." She saw his dark, shadowy figure stride quickly across the room, and a moment later the room was filled with a soft light. He had turned on a Tiffany lamp on a table. She received a quick impression of her surroundings: the ivory color of the velvet couch on which she was lying, gracious period furniture, green palms in a graceful vase in the corner, red roses in a milky white vase by the Tiffany lamp on the table, an impressionist painting of water lilies floating on a pond hanging on the wall opposite the couch.

Then her entire attention was caught and held by Louis. Standing naked and half turned away from her by the table, he had tight buttocks, a flat washboard stomach, a feathering of black hair on his chest, powerful thighs and calves. Dressed, he had been an elegant, graceful, extraordinarily handsome man, but now he was transformed; bold virility, sexual . . . and so beautiful she couldn't stop looking at him. She had the sudden urge to run her fingers through the rumpled black curls dipping untidily over his forehead.

He faced her, his eyes glittering in the lamplight. She was suddenly overcome with shyness. "I'd rather you turned off the light," she said.

"Why?" His expression was grim as he strolled back toward her. As he came closer she noticed the glitter of pale gold in the dark hair thatching his chest, a coin or medallion suspended from a rope-like gold chain, its barbaric richness enhancing the sensuality of his nudity. "You said later. This is later, isn't it?"

It was difficult to tear herself from this dreamy languor enveloping her. But she had to return to the world, his world—the real one, she supposed. "Yes, but I . . ." She trailed off as he stopped beside the couch, towering over her. "You're angry and I feel vulnerable."

"Good. That's exactly what I want you to feel. Maybe I'll get the truth for once. Why the hell didn't you tell me you were a virgin?"

She avoided his glance. "I didn't tell you I wasn't."

"Bull. You led me to believe you'd hopped in and out of more beds than you could count."

"You didn't seem to mind me being a virgin a few minutes ago."

He laughed harshly. "Hell, I went crazy. You were so damn tight I felt as if—" He broke off, his lips thinning. "You know how you made me feel. It's what you intended, right?"

"I hoped you'd have a pleasant experience." Her gaze shifted back to his face. "But my motives were principally selfish." She held up her hand as he opened his mouth to speak. "No, it didn't have anything to do with Muggins, Inc."

"I doubt that. What were you trying to do? Hang a guilt trip on me so it would be easier to gouge me during the negotiations?"

She shook her head and sat upright on the couch. "Will you please move out of the way? I'd like to get up and get dressed now."

"Lord, you're cool."

She suddenly looked up at him, her eyes blazing. "I'm *not* cool. I ache and I feel shaky and uncertain and I want to—"

"I hurt you?" he interrupted, frowning.

"A little. No more than I expected. May I get dressed?"

He muttered a curse beneath his breath, strode over to the gown lying in a heap on the floor, snatched it up, and carried it back to her. "Stand up."

She obediently got to her feet and stood still as he slipped the gown over her head. He turned her around and slid the zipper up the track. "Why?"

She sat down again and tucked her bare feet underneath her full taffeta skirt. The confrontation was coming but she wasn't sure she was ready for it. "Aren't you going to get dressed?"

"Do I embarrass you?" he asked sarcastically. "Is that why you made me leave the lights out?"

"No, that was for me. I knew it was going to be a fairly traumatic experience and I didn't know if I could keep in character," she said simply.

"'In character'?"

"I'm not saying I'm the most charismatic person in the world, but most people seem to find me likeable."

"So?"

"I knew I couldn't let you find me . . . sympathetic."

She could see the muscles of his shoulders tense. "And why not?

"Because you wouldn't have—" She said in a

rush, "You wouldn't have made love to a woman you liked. You can't equate sex with affection."

He stood motionless, his light eyes glittering in his set face.

She went on quickly, "I knew you'd be angry but I—"

"You're damned right I'm angry." His voice shook with fury. "How much did you pay Schuler?"

"Schuler?" She had to search her memory before she could place the name. "The psychiatrist you went to when you were a boy." She shook her head. "Don't blame him."

"I *do* blame him, for breaking a professional confidence. But I blame you a hell of a lot more for offering a bribe big enough to make him do it." His hands clenched into fists at his sides. "Damn you!"

"I didn't bribe—" It was easier to let him believe the breach of faith. "You have a perfect right to resent my probing into your personal life."

"How understanding. But it didn't stop you from doing it, did it? Just what did the bastard tell you?"

"I know you were a victim." She didn't want to see the anger in his face, so she fastened her gaze on the painting on the wall across the room. "From the time you were a little boy you were part of a gypsy street gang of pickpockets in Paris run by a professional criminal. When you were thirteen you were sold into a house of prostitution in Venice by the same man. You stayed there a year before the police broke up the ring and rescued you."

"Go on."

Dear God, this was difficult. "You went to Schuler when you were sixteen because you were having . . . problems." She kept her gaze on the picture. "You're exceptionally highly sexed and even at that age you needed a woman frequently. However, because of what happened to you in that place you resented your needs . . . when you made love to a woman you became . . . savage, a wild man. You exploded and went crazy." She added quickly, "Oh, I'm not talking about deliberate physical abuse. In fact, you never hurt anyone, but you came close to injuring your partners several times through loss of control. It scared you into going to Schuler."

"I wish I'd never seen the bigmouthed bastard now."

The bitterness in his tone sent a wave of pain through her. "He couldn't help you and the only thing he did was identify the problem. You were basically a very sensitive person and instinctively chose women you liked and respected to sleep with. The way you felt about sex and the affection you felt for your partners conflicted, releasing all the stored-up violence that—"

"I've heard enough."

"Since Schuler couldn't help, you found your own solution. You decided to keep any woman who aroused emotions of respect and affection at a distance and to go to bed with women who appealed to you only on a physical level, where no conflict existed. It was a compromise that allowed you to maintain control during the act, satisfy your sexual needs, and not endanger anyone."

"I said I'd heard enough."

She looked at his face once more and saw the implacable hardness she had expected. "I don't blame you for being angry. You're a very private person and it must seem as if I've violated you. I'd like to apologize."

"It's a little late for that."

"I don't expect you to forgive me. If the tables were turned, I'm not sure I could forgive. I merely wanted you to know." She got to her feet. "I'm going back to the house. I'm very tired and we have a lot of work to do tomorrow after the lawyers come."

"Not yet." His hand closed on her arm. "My Lord, you believe we're going merrily on with Muggins, Incorporated after this?"

"Of course." She gazed at him in surprise. "It will make you a bundle of money. Look, I could go to a number of people to get them to handle the production, or even handle it myself. My associates have no problem supplying either money or influence. But I'm not going to do it, because this is the only way I could think of to compensate you for what you did tonight."

"Compensate?" He laughed incredulously. "You sound like I'm a stud to be given extra grain for servicing a mare."

"I didn't mean—I told you I was awkward with words." She pulled away from him and walked quickly toward the door. "But you still have to do the deal. It's only right. I can't take something for nothing."

"Wait."

She stopped at the door and looked back at him.

"Why?" The violence in his soft voice vibrated in the still room. "Why all the manipulation, the probing? What do you need from me? *Why*, dammit?"

She knew it was the wrong time to tell him, but she was sick to death of lies. "A child," she whispered. "I need to have your child, Louis."

His eyes widened in shock. "What the hell—" He took a step forward.

"No more." He was too close. Nobody had ever been this close before, and it was frightening her. Her nerves were frayed to breaking and he kept coming closer and closer. . . . She had to end the confrontation. "Tomorrow. I'll talk to you tomorrow."

She turned and ran from the summerhouse, following the garden path toward the chateau.

A few minutes later she slammed the door of her bedroom behind her, locked it, and pressed her back against the polished panels.

It was done.

She should feel satisfaction, not this nagging ache, she told herself as she remembered Louis's expression in those moments before she had run out of the summerhouse. She had stripped away his armor, opened old wounds, hurt him, and it didn't help to tell herself she had been forced to do it, that there had been no choice. She was sharing every nuance of his pain as if it were her own.

And not only her emotions were raw; her body still felt a throbbing emptiness she knew was the same mindless desire for joining she had known before Louis had made love to her. She suddenly wanted to be back in the darkness moving under Louis as he thrust and thrust until . . .

Dear heaven, why did she still want him? She

had followed her plan down to the last detail. It should be over.

The desire had to be an aftereffect of the passion, she told herself. She would not think about it. She would go to bed and will herself to sleep.

She pushed away from the door and strode purposely toward the bathroom. She would take a hot shower to relax her and put her promptly to sleep.

She was sure the dream would not come tonight.

Three

"Good morning." Louis smiled sardonically as he watched her walk down the stairs the next morning. "I'm glad to say you look like hell. You had a bad night, I trust?"

Mariana's fingers flew to the black circles underscoring her eyes. "It wasn't good." She forced a smile. "Bad dreams."

He stiffened and an odd expression flickered over his face. "A guilty conscience?"

"No, I think it was Muggins's duck l'orange. It was too rich." She reached the bottom of the steps. "You don't look so bright-eyed yourself."

"What do you expect? You throw me into a turmoil and then run off into the night. I was tempted to break down your door and have it out with you."

"I thought you'd feel that way." She moved toward the study. "Okay, let's get it over with." She strode over to the leather chair by the fireplace, perched on the edge of the seat, and folded her hands on her lap. "I'm ready. Ask your questions."

He closed the door and leaned back against it. "The child."

"I want to have a baby. I'm twenty-four years old and I want someone of my own. I have a wonderful family and the Muggins, but that's not the same." She moistened her lips "There are times when I feel very . . . lonely."

"Do you expect me to be touched?"

"No, I know you're still angry. I simply feel you should know why I did it."

"It doesn't take a great deal of perceptiveness to realize I'm annoyed. I find every action you've taken verging on insanity."

"I wanted a child," she repeated. "Actually, I've tried to be very analytical and sensible about the problem."

"You'll forgive me if I disagree. And the man you chose to father this infant has no say in the matter?"

"Why should you mind? After we're finished with this business today I'll go back home and we'll never see each other again. It was just one night, and I won't ask any more from you."

"And may I ask why you selected me?"

She looked down at her folded hands. "I saw your picture on the cover of *Time*. You appealed to me."

He laughed incredulously. "Good Lord, I feel like a mail-order bride."

"Of course, I researched your background and found you were sound physically and mentally."

"Except for my little quirk."

"Actually, that only proved to me how strong you are. You faced a problem and found a way to solve it." She added earnestly, "Given your nature, I'm sure the solution wasn't to your complete satisfaction, but you've learned to live with the compromise."

"I seem to be perfect for your needs." His lips twisted. "And you're sure one night will be enough?"

"Last night was biologically perfect for conception. I tested myself this morning with the kit I got from my doctor, and I don't believe there's any reason why I would have to bother you again."

"How comforting." He moved away from the door and came toward her, graceful, catlike, menacing. She instinctively stiffened, and he smiled mirthlessly. "Are you afraid? You damn well should be. For such a clever lady, you've made a very big mistake. All that information and you still didn't put together an accurate picture of me."

"What do you mean?"

"One, I hate being used." His hands grasped her shoulders and he yanked her to her feet. "That's one of the things I learned when I was in that charming dwelling in Venice. Two, I had such a lousy childhood myself that there's no way I'd let a calculating opportunist go away carrying my child without keeping tabs on her." His white teeth bared in a savage smile. "And three, I ardently believe in the old adage 'An eye for an eye.'"

"I didn't totally disregard the possibility that—" She gasped as his grip tightened bruisingly on her shoulders. "You're hurting me."

His grip lessened fractionally, but his tone lowered to lethal silkiness. "Then that proves you were wrong about another facet of my character. According to you, I shouldn't have any trouble controlling my emotions with a woman I dislike." His left hand moved up to stroke her cheek. "But perhaps you're the exception to prove the rule. You'll notice that last night, for the first time in years, I almost lost control while I was making love to a woman."

Her uneasiness was instantly submerged by curiosity. "Did you? At one point you were very . . . intense, but I thought perhaps the roughness was usual in these circumstances. Why do you suppose you had that reaction?"

"What diff—" He frowned and shook his head. "That damn analytical mind."

"I can't help it," she said defensively.

"That you think like a robot and have just as much emotion?"

"You're not being reasonable. If I had less emotion I wouldn't have come here. I told you, I want a child."

"And why didn't you involve yourself in a normal relationship instead of choosing a man from a photograph?"

She was silent, her hands opening and closing nervously at her sides.

"No answer?"

"I didn't . . . It was necessary that I . . ." She drew a deep breath and then burst out, "Why do you think you're the only one with problems? I *can't* have a so-called normal relationship. I had to do it this way."

"Why?"

She shook her head.

"You won't answer?"

"I can't answer." She looked up at him pleadingly. "There are things I can't tell you. I knew I shouldn't have said a word to you about the child but I wanted to be as honest as I could with you."

"There are too damn many questions you won't answer. You appear out of nowhere and offer me a deal too good to be true and then proceed to totally disrupt my life. I ask you for reasons and you give me only vague generalities and evasions." His voice was very soft. "Now that's not fair, Mariana. You know everything about me and let me learn nothing about you."

"I wasn't vague about Muggins, Inc."

"Ah, Muggins, Inc. . . . My reward for being a good stud."

"It wasn't like—well, perhaps it was a little, but I—"

"You're stammering. Have I have managed to disconcert you?"

She gazed up at him defiantly. "Of course you have. You're hovering over me like Dracula about to draw a half-pint and you expect me not to be nervous?"

"A full pint. And you've seen to it that I don't know *what* to expect of you." He smiled. "But that's going to change. I'm going to get to know your every secret. Before we're done no one on earth is going to know you as well as I do. You're going to be made to feel as vulnerable and exposed as you've made me feel."

"I never wanted to make you feel this way," she said desperately. "Believe me, I tried for weeks to think of any other course I could follow that would solve my problem without—"

"Why should I believe you? You've deceived me from the minute you marched into my garden." He released her and stepped back. "But I'm not having any more of it. No lies, no deceit. Only the truth. Count on it." He turned and moved toward the door. "Don't try to leave Darceaubeau. I've given orders to my security people that you're not to be permitted to depart until I say the word."

Her eyes widened. "You're keeping me prisoner?"

"I believe that's an accurate term." He opened the door. "By the way, how did you get onto the grounds? The guards said no one entered or left through the front gate."

"Well, if I didn't come through the gate, how do you know I can't leave the same way I got in?"

"Because I'll have men patrolling the grounds from now on." He added, "Accompanied by two very well-trained and quite ferocious Dobermans."

She shook her head dazedly. "You really mean it. This is ridiculous. When your lawyers arrive, I'm sure they'll lecture you on the dangers of criminal behavior."

"I called Paris this morning and canceled the meeting." He glanced back over his shoulder. "Before cutting the phone lines. I want us to be entirely undisturbed while we become better acquainted."

She felt a sudden jolt of fear as she realized she

wouldn't be able to call Gunner tomorrow night. "Don't do this."

"Would you care to reconsider and tell me the truth?"

"I can't. You wouldn't understand."

"I'm not unintelligent, Mariana. I might not be sympathetic, but I'd understand."

"No." She took a step toward him. "You mustn't do this. It's not safe for you to keep me here against my will."

He smiled mockingly. "Are you threatening me?"

"I'm trying to talk sense to you. It's dangerous for you, Louis."

"I'll risk it."

She started to protest again but he had already closed the door behind him.

Louis went immediately to the kitchen, flipped up the two-way switch of the intercom on the wall, and punched the button labeled *G* for gate.

"Hendricks?"

"What can I do for you, Mr. Benoit?"

"Send one of the men to the Paris office and talk to Paul Girard. Tell him to call Randolph's Investigative Agency in New York and get them on this. I want to know everything there is to know about the woman who is our guest this weekend. Got a pen?"

"Yes."

"Mariana Sandell, age twenty-four, five feet two, dark hair, brown eyes, a scientist who specializes in robotics. Arrived at DeGaulle yesterday morning."

"From where?"

"How the hell do I know? That's why we're calling Randolph's." He was about to press the "close" switch when he remembered something. "Compound. She said she lived in a compound. Not a military compound. She described it as sort of a town. And it's not in the U.S. or France."

"You told us to cut the phone lines. How do we get the report?"

"Send a man into the office twice a day until he has something to bring back."

"Mr. Benoit." Hendricks's tone was hesitant. "I don't want to get into trouble with the authorities. Are you sure keeping her here isn't a bit . . . extreme?"

"I'll take full responsibility. Get on it." He pressed the "disconnect" switch.

Extreme. The man was right—the actions he had taken were extreme, but so were all the emotions Mariana engendered in him. From the first she had amused and intrigued him, and lust had quickly followed. Last night in the summerhouse he had been dangerously close to falling off the tightrope he had walked all these years, and the fury he had felt later had not lessened but escalated his desire for her. While she had been sitting in that big chair in the library, looking like an earnest little girl as she explained why she had tricked him into making love to her, he had been remembering how tight she had felt around him, the sounds she had made as she—

"And a grand morning to you, Mr. Benoit."

He whirled away from the intercom to see Mrs.

Muggins gliding toward him. He stiffened defensively as he recalled that Muggins had been programmed to obey Mariana. Then he relaxed. He had examined the blueprints himself and Mrs. Muggins's program absolutely forbade violence of any sort. "Good morning."

"I'll be serving your breakfast on the terrace in twenty minutes. Croissants, orange juice, and coffee?"

"No, thank you."

"You must eat." She glided toward the refrigerator. "You must keep up your strength for the trials ahead."

"What trials are you—"

"Run along to the terrace." Mrs. Muggins began humming "When Irish Eyes Are Smiling" as her metal digits deftly extracted cartons of orange juice and milk from the shelf and deposited them on the countertop.

"I told you I didn't want breakfast."

"Twenty minutes." She reached for the coffee canister on the counter.

Louis shook his head and turned and left the kitchen. He had no intention of meekly obeying the robot and going to the terrace. Instead, he would go to the garden and sit for a while and try to calm himself. Lord knew, he needed quieting.

Mariana picked up the receiver of the phone on her nightstand. No dial tone. She hadn't thought Louis was bluffing but she had to check. She returned the receiver to the cradle.

Damn, she had messed up everything.

When she had made the decision to deceive Louis, she should have gone the distance. But no, she had to soothe her conscience by telling him as much of the truth as she felt safe revealing—and had made him even more furious with her.

But no matter how angry he was, she hadn't thought he would do this. She supposed she shouldn't have been surprised. Andrew had warned her about the volatility below Louis's composed facade.

Gunner.

Dammit, she *had* to get out of here. From childhood she had witnessed Gunner's ruthlessness and deadly efficiency. He was a legend among the Clanad and she had no intention of turning that legend loose on Louis. She had taken away enough from him.

So she had to find a way of getting to a telephone by tomorrow evening, when Gunner would be expecting her call.

The gate would be impassable, since she had no one to help her this time and the grounds of the chateau were enclosed by a stone wall towering over sixteen feet. She had only given the wall a passing glance, but it had appeared smooth, with no noticeable ridges where one could gain a hold.

Blast it, there had to be some way she could get over that stone wall. Of course, she would have to leave Mrs. Muggins and take nothing but her passport and money belt . . .

Tonight. She would wait until after midnight and make the attempt

• • •

No moonlight.

She tried to suppress a shiver of apprehension as she hurried down the walk through the rose garden. She supposed she should have been grateful, but moonlight would still have been comforting, in spite of its dangers. She had always been afraid of the dark.

The wall was directly ahead.

Mariana broke into a trot, her gaze fixed on the white blur a hundred yards ahead. A gnarled, ancient oak tree grew a short distance from the stone wall and its lower branches hovered about five feet above the top of the wall. If she could shinny up and gain purchase perhaps she could work her way hand over hand to the top of the wall, drop down, and then—

Then what?

Humpty-Dumpty sat on a wall
Humpty-Dumpty had a great fall . . .

The lines of the children's verse suddenly popped into her mind.

Nonsense, she would be fine. Though she spent most of her time in the laboratory she was physically fit and there was no reason why she wouldn't be able to do it.

She would worry about getting down on the other side when she reached the top. If worse came to worst, she could always hang by her hands and risk dropping to the ground. It couldn't be—

Dogs!

She stopped, her gaze searching the darkness.

The shrill barking was coming from the front of the chateau but that didn't mean the patrol wouldn't be back in the garden in a few minutes.

She broke into a run, reaching the oak tree in seconds. The next minute she was shinnying up the tree. By the time she reached the lower branches she was breathless, her heart pounding wildly from exertion, her palms lacerated and bleeding from contact with the rough bark.

She wiped her cut palms on her jeans as she balanced astride a branch. Six feet and she would reach the top of the wall. All she had to do was grasp the branch and go hand over hand until she was directly over the wall and then drop down onto its flat surface.

She took a deep breath, grasped the branch, and let her weight drop until she hung suspended.

Barking!

Closer.

She started moving hand over hand, her arms hurting, straining.

A trickle of blood ran down her left wrist from one of the open cuts on her palm.

The dogs were closer and she could hear men's voices now.

The barking suddenly became excited yelping!

Had she been seen by the men? Scented by the dogs?

Dear Lord, she was only halfway across.

She moved faster.

The yelping was closer, almost on top of her.

Below her!

She reached desperately for the next handhold on the branch.

"What the hell!"

A light pierced the darkness, blinding her.

She missed the handhold!

She was falling . . .

Pain exploded in her left temple!

Darkness.

She looked so . . . little.

Crumpled on the ground beneath the tree, she appeared no more than a child. With all that vitality and nervous energy dimmed, she was a very helpless child.

"I checked her over after I sent for you and I don't think there are any broken bones, Mr. Benoit."

Louis never took his gaze from Mariana. "I told you not to hurt her," he said hoarsely.

"It was an accident. The dogs scented something and we—"

"Send for the doctor in the village. I want him here in half an hour, and tell him to bring portable X-ray equipment." He knelt beside Mariana. Her hands were bleeding, he noticed dully.

Guilt and pain exploded inside him. Guilt, and pain, and another emotion he had been afraid to recognize. An emotion that had been there, underlying everything that had gone between them, since the moment she had walked toward him in this very garden.

He gathered her into his arms and stood up. "Don't stand there. Get that doctor!"

• • •

She was being carried up stairs.

Pain shot through her head at every step, but at least she was awake. Pain was better than what waited for her in the darkness.

Her lids slowly opened.

Crystal-gray eyes. Louis's eyes.

"Louis?" she whispered.

He looked down at her. "Be quiet." His voice was thick. "You hit your head, but it's going to be all right. I'll make it all right."

"Humpty-Dumpty broke his crown . . ."

"You didn't break—" He stopped and then started again. "I'll fix it!"

His tone vibrated with such determination she was forced to believe him. Anyway, she was too woozy to argue and she had to use all her strength to fight the darkness that was closing in again. "Dark."

His stride was smooth now. They were going down the hall. "Dear God, you're stiff as a board. Stop fighting. Let go. I'll take care of you."

"You can't. Alone. No one can help . . ."

"You're not alone. I'm here."

"You'll go away. You always go away." Her fingers dug into his shoulder, but she was already losing him. "I wake up and you're not there."

"Shhh." He laid her on the bed. "You're hurt and not making sense."

She was making sense, but he didn't understand. He didn't understand what waited in the dark. It was getting closer! Panic tightened around her chest until she couldn't breathe.

"Relax." Louis's voice was hoarse. "You look like you're being stretched on a rack. I can't take this." He held her hand. "Let me help you."

She clutched desperately at his hand.

Warmth. Safety. Strength.

She was so tired of fighting. Perhaps Louis was strong enough to pull her from the abyss.

She let the darkness overwhelm her.

Four

Gray eyes again only inches away, shimmering in the lamplight.

No, not lamplight, she realized hazily; it was sunlight streaming through the windows of her room.

"Morning," she whispered.

"Afternoon." Louis leaned forward and gently brushed a tendril of hair from her forehead. "You've been unconscious since last night."

She had been hurt. Bandages on her hands . . . the tree. But she was safe now with Louis. She was back in her room at the chateau, dressed in her own cotton nightgown.

"The doctor was worried. He was sure it was only a mild concussion and shouldn't have caused such a trauma."

She closed her eyes as she remembered the smothering fear that had invaded her every pore last night. "It was . . . dark."

"You kept repeating that. You held on to my hand and kept saying it over and over."

She was still holding his hand, she realized, clasping it so tightly she must be hurting him. Her lids flew open and she jerked her hand away. "I'm sorry."

"*You're* sorry?" His voice was rough. "You fell out of my damned tree, trying to get away from my security people, and you're sorry? I was ready to kill someone when I saw you lying there on the ground. I told them not to hurt you. I told them to stop you, but not to—"

"They didn't hurt me. It was the light. Someone turned on the flashlight and the beam blinded me and I missed my grip. Don't blame them."

"You're always saying that. Don't blame the gate guards, don't blame Schuler; now I'm not supposed to blame—" He stopped. "You're right. There's no one to blame but myself. I gave the orders and it's my fault you were hurt."

"It wasn't your fault either. You warned me."

"And that makes everything fine? For Lord's sake, I put you in a prison. Of course it was my fault if something happened to you when you tried to escape. When I saw you lying there . . ." He shook his head. "I felt like a murderer."

"Don't be ridiculous. I set up the situation and I fully expected to take the consequences." She struggled to a sitting position. *Pain.* She quickly leaned back against the headboard. "Oops."

"Are you all right?"

"Fine," she murmured.

"The hell you are. I'll get the sedative the doctor left for you."

"No!" She saw his eyes narrow speculatively and quickly tempered her tone. "I've slept enough. I'm going to get up."

"No." His expression was implacable. "You're staying right where you are. Blast it, the doctor was within an inch of taking you to the hospital last night."

"I told you I was fine." She glared at him belligerently. "I'm never sick and I hate lying about doing nothing."

"Then you shouldn't go around cracking your head open."

"I didn't . . ." She grimaced. "What a disgusting expression. It brings all kinds of unpleasant pictures to mind."

"Yes, it does." He stood up. "And I don't want to remember any of them. Stay where you are and I'll get Mrs. Muggins to fix you some invalid fare."

"Don't do that. She'll be in here fussing over me." She frowned. "I'm surprised she hasn't been here already."

"I told her to stay out. She was getting in my way."

"And she obeyed you? Hmmm . . ."

He started for the door. "It's a good thing she did. I was in a mood to break something last night."

She tried to smile. "Then it was a blessing I was already broken."

He whirled to face her. "It's nothing to joke about, dammit. When I first saw you lying there I thought I'd killed you."

She couldn't cope with the waves of emotion she was receiving from him. She quickly lowered her gaze and said flippantly, "You were certainly angry enough with me to do just that. I would have thought you'd be relieved that I'd saved you the trouble."

"Then you'd have been wrong." His words were halting. "I never wanted to hurt you."

"Then you're going to let me go?"

He said quickly, "You're not well enough."

"But after I'm better?"

"We'll talk about it later."

Later might be too late, she remembered suddenly. Gunner!

"Louis!"

He paused at the door and looked back at her.

"I have to make a telephone call."

"I can't get the telephone lines repaired until Monday." He smiled lopsidedly. "As usual, it's much easier to destroy than to build."

"Then I'll have to go to the village and place the call."

"You're not leaving your bed," he said flatly.

"I *have* to make that call."

"I'll make it for you. Give me the number and the message."

"I can't. He'll want to know why I didn't place the call myself and if you tell him I'm hurt he'll—"

"Him?"

Louis had stiffened, and she could sense the tension her words had created. "Who do you want to call? Your father?"

"No."

"A lover?" He smiled again. "If so, he won't be any more pleased about our little rendezvous in the summerhouse than I was. We primitive males enjoy being first. Does he know why you came here?"

"No, and that's why I have to—" His expression was hardening more by the second, and she gazed at him helplessly. "Please let me make the call and I'll come right back to the chateau and go to bed."

"He'll have to wait until Monday." Louis's tone was harsh. "I'm afraid you'll have to rely on me to amuse you for the next few days."

He closed the door with such force it was almost a slam.

Dear heavens, he was stubborn.

She glanced at the clock on the nightstand by the bed. It was three twenty-five. Gunner would be expecting her to call by eight. He would probably give her no more than four hours' grace and would be on his way from Sedikhan to Darceaubeau by midnight.

She swung her legs to the floor and carefully stood up. Her knees immediately buckled and she fell back on the bed.

Damn! Her clenched hand pounded the mattress in frustration.

She was too weak to put on her clothes, much less try to escape the chateau.

But she wouldn't stay this way. She would eat every bit of the lunch Louis had brought her and rest and gain strength. Then, if she still couldn't persuade Louis to take her to the village, she would have no choice but to make another attempt at that blasted wall.

"You did very well." Louis picked up her tray and set it on the floor beside the bed. "Judging by the dinner you ate the other night I thought you were one of those women who pick at their food."

"I usually have a good appetite. I was scared that night." She leaned back against the headboard. "I expected every minute for you to call my bluff."

"It would have served you right if I had." He took the napkin and dabbed at her mouth. "You shouldn't throw out invitations if you don't expect them to be accepted. You're lucky my tastes aren't particularly kinky."

"Well, I had to get your attention. I'm no gorgeous vamp like the women you usually—" She broke off and tilted her head to study him. "You're not angry with me any longer, are you?"

"Do you want a cloth to wash your face?"

"Later. Why aren't you mad at me?"

He leaned back in his chair. "You scared it out of me. It's amazing how guilt can—"

"I told you that you weren't guilty. I'm the one who was responsible." She smiled tentatively. "But I'm glad you're not angry any longer. It . . . bothered me."

"Why should my attitude matter to you? You got what you wanted." His tone lowered. "Or did you?"

"Of course I did," she said staunchly. "I told you—"

"Practically nothing," he finished. "And managed to hit me in such a vulnerable spot I couldn't see anything but my own pain and anger . . ." He paused. "And lust." He saw her stiffen and smiled faintly. "Yes, oh yes, it's still there—perhaps stronger than ever. But don't worry. I had a long time to think while I watched you sleep last night."

"And?"

"I remembered my first impression of you, before anything else got in the way." He looked down at her bandaged hand on the coverlet. "A brave child full of spirit and determination, one I could like. You know me well enough to know I never run the risk of sleeping with someone I like."

"I'm not a child."

"No? Yet I think you still have much of the child in you. You're curious and idealistic and still afraid of the dark. Do you know that you held my hand as if I were your last anchor in the world? Even when you were unconscious you wouldn't let me go."

"I'm sorry."

"You shouldn't be. You completely disarmed me." His index finger lightly stroked her knuckle. "And made me remember what you said about your own problems. What problems, *ma petite*?"

She shook her head.

A brilliant smile lit his features. "We're going to be partners, and I could be a very good friend to you as well, Mariana. Trust me."

He was warm as sunlight, as beautiful as Apollo, drawing her to him. She impulsively turned over her hand and grasped his.

Safety. Warmth. Companionship.

His grasp tightened. "Trust me. I know what it is to be frightened and alone."

Yes, Louis knew. She felt the tears sting her eyes as she remembered what a nightmare his childhood had been. Yet he had survived it and let his past hurt only himself. "I'd like to tell you."

"Then talk to me." The pad of his thumb rubbed

gently back and forth across the top of her hand. "Tell me how I can help you."

She shook her head. "You wouldn't understand."

"You said that before." He reached out and tucked a curl behind her ear. "And I told you that you were wrong." He released her hand. "But I can wait; I'm a very patient man." He grimaced. "I've had to be."

She glanced at the clock on the table. Five-thirty. Two and a half hours before she was due to telephone Gunner. "I really feel much better. Couldn't you take me to the village to call—"

"No!" His expression hardened in the space of a heartbeat. "You'll have to wait to phone your—" He stopped and a bitter smile curved his lips. "What do I call him? He's not your lover, at least in the carnal sense. *I* had that honor. It's only—Oh, for heaven's sake, stop looking at me like that."

"How am I looking at you?"

"As if I were . . ." He stood up and moved toward the cabinet across the room. "I'll turn on the television set and let you stare at something else for a change. Or perhaps you'll nap. It would be much better for you."

"I don't want to sleep."

"I didn't think so. You seem to have an aversion to it." He turned on the television and took the remote from the top of the cabinet. "Then be quiet and stare at the boob tube. Considering the quality of offerings on the small screen these days it should put you to sleep whether you want to or not." He dropped down into the chair beside her bed. "I'll be right here if you decide you want to say something to me besides 'You wouldn't understand, Louis.'"

Six fifty-five.

Mariana looked away from the clock as she felt Louis's gaze on her face. "I'm tired of watching television." She shifted restlessly against the pillows. "I should be working. Will you bring me the yellow scratch pad on top of the bureau?"

"I'm hurt. Haven't I proved amusing enough for you?"

He had been *too* entertaining. She had completely forgotten the passage of time until she had happened to glance at the clock. "Of course, but I must get to work. You don't have to baby-sit me. If you'll just get me the pad I'll—"

"I will not," Louis said firmly. "You don't have to work every minute of every day."

"Why not? *You* do."

"Not at Darceaubeau."

She tilted her head to look at him. "Why did you choose Darceaubeau for your sanctuary?"

"It's where my roots are. Don't we always go back to our roots?"

"I don't know." Her nervous fingers began creasing and uncreasing the top sheet. "I guess I've never thought much about it. My roots have always been my work and my family, not a particular place."

"But I have no family, and work can exhaust as well as satisfy. You'll find that out as you grow older."

She grimaced. "Yes, grandpa."

He smiled. "Was I being patronizing?"

"A little. But I'm used to it. When you're a touch over five feet tall people tend to forget you're a woman, not a child. In the summerhouse I wasn't even sure you would want to—" She broke off as she saw where her thoughtless words were leading. She hadn't meant to mention what had happened in the summerhouse, dammit. She could feel the heat sting her cheeks and ended lamely, "I mean, I knew you like women who are more . . ." She trailed off and wondered desperately why she couldn't shut up.

"More what?"

"Just more."

"I found you entirely adequate." His bearing was no longer relaxed. "I believe we'd better talk about something else."

"Fine." Her fingers plucked at the plateaus of the creases she had made on the sheet. "You don't have to stay here with me. Don't you have something to do?"

"Stop that." His hand covered hers on the sheet, stilling the feverish activity. "What are you so nervous about?"

She was suddenly award of the tension charging the air between them, the same electricity that had been present in the summerhouse before he had come to her in the darkness.

"I need something to do. If you'd get my pad I could—"

"That's not why you're nervous. Is it me?"

She didn't look at him. "Partly, I suppose."

"I told you that you didn't have to worry. I've

placed you in an entirely new category. You're out-of-bounds."

She didn't feel out-of-bounds. His grip on her hand was warm, possessive, and generated a tingling throughout her body. Her breasts were swelling, the tips pushing against the cotton of her nightgown.

"I realize that." She was astonished to discover she was trembling. He was merely holding her hand and her body was reacting as if he were seducing her. "It's only that—"

"I know." His voice was thick. "I can feel it. Dear Lord, how I can feel it." He released her hand. "But it won't happen. I won't let it happen. I promise you." He abruptly pushed back his chair and stood up. "I think it's time I took a walk."

"Where are you going?"

"I don't know. I'll be back soon."

"Could I have my work pad?"

"What a bulldog you are." He moved toward the door, his stride jerky. "No, you can't work. You'll have to be satisfied with the television." He gave her a stern glance. "And you're not to move from that bed."

She watched the door close behind him and experienced an explosive release of tension. The erotic awareness had come out of nowhere and caught her off guard. He had warned her it was still there but had kept it so well hidden she had not been conscious of it until the instant he had touched her.

Oh yes, then she had definitely been conscious of it. She was still suffering the aftereffects. Her body felt empty, aching. A vision of Louis standing

naked by the Tiffany lamp in the summerhouse
came back to her and she tensed as she realized it
was the solution to the need her body was tele-
graphing.

She blocked the thought, staring blindly at the
flickering television screen. When she had come
here everything had seemed so clear, but now she
was becoming confused and uncertain.

Still another reason to get away from Darceaubeau as soon as possible.

"Hot milk," Louis said as he entered her bedroom a short time later. His expression was bland
and controlled, as if he hadn't stalked out of the
room only a little more than an hour before. He
carried the glass over to the bed. "Mrs. Muggins
insists."

"I hate hot milk." Mariana glanced surrepti-
tiously at the clock on the bedside table. Eight
forty-five. She could picture Gunner sitting in his
study in the Compound waiting for the call.

"Drink it anyway. I'm in enough trouble with our
robotic friend."

Mariana took the glass and looked at him over
the rim. "She's actually being quite docile. I don't
understand it."

"Perhaps she knows I'm only doing what's best
for you." He sat down in the chair he had occupied
all afternoon and smiled at her. "I wish you'd
realize I'm no longer a threat to you, Mariana."

He was more of a threat to her now than he had
been at his angriest. He had laughed with her,
teased her, wrapped her in a warm cocoon of

tenderness from which she was having trouble freeing herself. She was truly getting to know him—the ultimate danger. There had been moments this afternoon when she had felt so close to him. "You're being . . . very kind to me."

"I have an idea I'm not the only one who has an ugly past to shake off." He straightened the covers around her with the protectiveness of a mother tucking in a beloved child. "Who made you a victim, Mariana?"

"No one." With an effort, she smiled. "You're wrong—I have had a perfect childhood, parents who love me, no economic worries, a wonderful, affectionate home life."

"It sounds too good to be true." He met her gaze. "I believe you're lying to me. I've seen too many walking wounded not to recognize one when she barges into my life."

She glanced at the clock again. Eight fifty-five. She had to get Louis out of her room. She had no idea how long, given her weakened condition, it would take to dress and make her way from the chateau to the village. "I'm tired," she said abruptly. "You can leave me now. Good night."

He lifted his brows. "Dismissed?"

"Thank you, but I'm fine. You need your rest too."

"Does that mean you're tired of my company?"

She wished it did. She was finding his presence perilously sweet. "I'm just accustomed to being alone."

"All right. Drink your milk and I'll leave you to your solitude."

She quickly drained the glass. "Ugh."

He laughed. "What a face. It can't be that bad."

He looked surprisingly boyish when he laughed, she thought dreamily. As if all the ugliness and unhappiness he had experienced had never touched him. But it *had* touched him, hurt him. Sweet heaven, she wished she could erase those experiences, ease his hurt. The passionate intensity of that desire shocked her and sent a surge of fear spiraling through her. Close. Too close.

"I told you I hated hot milk." She feigned a yawn and scooted down in the bed. "Good night."

He leaned over, then pressed a butterfly kiss on her forehead. The scent of lemon and . . . Louis. "*Bonne nuit, ma petite.*"

"You didn't speak French when we first met." This time the yawn was real. "But in the summerhouse . . ."

"We always fall back on the language of our childhood when we're in the throes of emotion or among friends."

His crystal-gray eyes were shimmering above her. Beautiful, wise, sad eyes. "You keep calling me your friend but . . ." She yawned again. "You were so angry. I can't understand why . . ." She trailed off as she forgot what she had been saying.

He stroked her hair back from her temple. "I discovered something . . . disturbing when I saw you lying unconscious."

"What?"

"Never mind. Go to sleep."

No, she had to stay awake; and besides, she had an idea he was saying something important. "What?"

"It doesn't matter. You said I was a man who

could compromise. It's become clear I cannot let you go out of my life, so I must compromise."

"But I have to go . . ." Why was she so sleepy? Only a moment ago she had been wide awake. She forced her lids to stay open. He was sitting back down in the chair beside her bed. That was wrong. She had told him he had to leave. "Go . . ."

He shook his head. "You'll be asleep in a moment. The sedative was strong, so I doubt if you'll stir tonight. But I still want to be here in case you need me."

"Sedative." Her voice sounded slurred as her glance flew to the empty glass on the nightstand. "No!"

"The doctor said you needed rest, and you've been fighting taking a nap all afternoon. You have to sleep tonight."

Gunner!

She struggled to sit up. "I can't—You'll—hurt—"

He pushed her back onto the pillows. "I'm right here." He grabbed her hand and held tightly. "Stop panicking. Nothing's going to hurt you."

Not me. You!

She thought she had screamed the words, but no sound had come from her lips. Her lids were fluttering, shutting as if weighted.

"Easy." His voice was a velvet murmur as the darkness closed down around her. "I won't leave you. I'll never leave you. . . ."

Five

No!

Her mouth stretched wide in a silent scream as wave after wave of agony swept over her. She went rigid on the bed; every atom of her being seemed to burn, tear.

Why?

Then, somewhere beneath the torturous whirl-pool, something shifted, became clear. Though it felt as if she were feeling every nuance of the pain, it was really only an echo. The pain was not her own.

Louis's pain!

Her eyes flew open. "Gunner!"

Her gaze flew to the chair beside the bed. Empty. She had known Louis wouldn't be there.

Another wave of pain washed over her.

She threw aside the covers and staggered to her feet. "No," she whimpered. "No, Gunner, don't . . ."

He couldn't hear her. They were downstairs in

the foyer. Louis was lying on the floor, fighting Gunner, fighting the pain. Gunner was standing over him, a savage smile of satisfaction on his face.

She stumbled to the door, down the hall.

Then she was standing on the top step looking down at the sight in the foyer she had known she would see.

"Gunner." Her whisper wasn't loud enough for him to hear and he was concentrating too intently on Louis to realize she was watching.

She would have to go down . . .

She held on to the railing with both hands as she started down the steps.

Dear heaven, if only the pain would stop.

"Gunner, please." She might as well save her strength—Gunner couldn't hear her. He was frowning; Louis was causing him problems.

Another step. Then another. She was only two steps away from the foyer.

Louis. Poor Louis. If her agony was only an echo, what must he be feeling?

She let go of the banister and staggered across the foyer toward Louis.

"Stop—Gunner."

Gunner whirled to face her, his gaze raking her strained features. "Mariana, what the hell are—"

"Stop." She dropped down on the floor beside Louis and reached out to cradle him in her arms, rocking him back and forth. "Hurts—Gunner. Hurts so much . . ."

"Dear Lord, I had no idea, Mariana," Gunner muttered. "You know I wouldn't—He's so strong—I didn't know—"

Suddenly the pain was gone, and with it the

feeble strength that had sustained her. She felt numbed, dazed with weariness. She was scarcely conscious of Louis's body stirring against her.

He raised his head. "Mariana?"

Gunner took a step toward them.

With lightning speed Louis rolled out of her arms and struggled to his knees, his eyes blazing at Gunner. "Stay away from her, you bastard."

Gunner halted in place. "I won't hurt her." He wearily ran his fingers through his silver-streaked hair. "Any more than I already have. It seems I misunderstood the situation."

"So the minute I open the front door you attack me. What the hell did you use on me?"

"I was angry and worried about Mariana." Gunner shrugged. "I told you to hurt."

"Told me to . . ." Louis gazed at him in astonishment before turning back to Mariana. "I don't have time to listen to any more of this bizarre nonsense. I've got to get her back to bed."

They were talking about her as if she weren't there, Mariana thought remotely. Perhaps they were right. She felt as if she were standing somewhere outside her body and watching them all. She wanted to go to sleep, but had to hold on until she was sure Gunner wasn't going to hurt Louis again.

Louis picked her up in his arms and started up the staircase.

"She's bandaged. What happened to her?" Gunner asked as he followed Louis up the stairs.

"Accident. Minor concussion. I gave her a sedative strong enough to knock out a grizzly bear a few hours ago to make her sleep. I don't know how the devil she even managed to get out of bed."

"Really?" Gunner's tone was thoughtful. "Unusual. Under those circumstances she should never have been affected."

"I don't know what the hell you're talking about," Louis said roughly. "But I wish you'd get out of here. I'll take care of her. She doesn't need you."

"How fierce you are." Gunner smiled. "Sorry. I can't go anywhere without talking to Mariana. Andrew needs a report." His gaze shifted to Mariana's face. "And she's in no shape to talk now."

"Gunner, don't hurt . . ." She trailed off as Gunner put two fingers on her lips.

"It's all right. You can go to sleep. I wouldn't dare touch him now that I know the situation."

"Promise?" she whispered.

He frowned. "When have we ever needed promises between us?"

"Promise."

"I promise."

It was all right. Louis was safe. She could let go now.

She let the numbness take her, flow over her as she relaxed in Louis's arms. A few minutes later he set her down on her bed and tucked the covers around her.

"You're probably suffering some pretty severe aftereffects, Benoit. I'll stay with her," Gunner said.

"The devil you will." Louis's tone turned fierce. "Evidently she knows you, so you can find yourself a room until she wakes up. But don't come near her without me being here."

"I'm not going to hurt her. Blast it, I was the one who sat up all night with her when she had chicken pox. I taught her to ride her first bicycle."

"Go find yourself a room."

Gunner chuckled. "It seems you're both obsessed with protecting each other from me. By the way, my name is Gunner Nilsen and I happen to be Mariana's godfather." He gently touched Mariana's cheek with his finger. "Good night, kid. We'll talk in the morning."

Louis looked exhausted, Mariana realized the moment she opened her eyes the next afternoon. Dark bags bruised the puffy flesh beneath his eyes, both contrasting with and underscoring the unhealthy pallor of his complexion.

"You look terrible," she said. "For Lord's sake, go get some rest."

"I'm not tired." He grimaced as he met her skeptical stare. "Well, maybe a little." He cautiously flexed the muscles of his shoulders. "Whatever your godfather hit me with made me ache in every joint of my body."

"Then go take a hot bath and grab a nap."

He shook his head. "I'll stay."

She gazed at him in exasperation. "For pity's sake, stop hovering over me. I'm probably in better shape than you are right now. Usually the men Gunner gets angry with are incapacitated for weeks."

"Interesting. And just who is this Gunner Nilsen?"

"He's a sort of policeman."

"Under what jurisdiction?"

"We'll talk about it later."

His lips tightened. "I want answers, Mariana. I think I deserve them."

"So do I," she said wearily. "You'll get your answers, but not until you're rested and capable of thinking with a clear head."

"Or I 'won't understand'?"

"You probably won't understand anyway, but I might have at least a chance of getting through to you."

"And how do I know you won't leave while I'm asleep?"

"I'm not going anywhere. It's too late. Between us, Gunner and I have blown it royally. We've both hurt you and now we have to make amends."

He gazed at her searchingly for a moment before nodding slowly. "Okay. I'm not about to refuse any bones you choose to toss my way, if it keeps you here. I'll see you in a few hours." He started toward the door. "Stay in bed and rest. I'll send Mrs. Muggins up with your lunch."

"Will you stop taking care of me?"

He gave her a ghost of a smile. "Probably not. It's becoming a habit."

She waited for the door to close behind him before tossing the covers aside and getting out of bed. Her knees still felt a bit quivery, but on the whole she found she was a good deal stronger than she had been the day before—and she certainly couldn't lie in bed and think. What had happened last night had too many frightening ramifications for her to decipher. She would keep busy and block it all out until the fear went away. She made her way slowly toward the bathroom.

An hour later she had showered and dressed and was about to go in search of Gunner when a knock sounded on the door. The knock was immediately followed by Gunner's entrance.

"Good afternoon." He appraised her swiftly. "You look alive again. Last night you resembled a zombie."

"That's what I felt like." She grimaced. "I'm still a bit weak in the knees."

"No other side effects?"

"Soreness in the joints."

"That's common in these cases. Sit down. We have some chatting to do."

"Agreed." She sat down on the cushioned window seat. "This shouldn't have happened, Gunner."

"You didn't call. You knew what to expect."

"I *couldn't* call."

"How were you hurt?"

"It was an accident." She added evasively, "I had a fall."

"Where?"

"In the garden."

"You're not usually clumsy. How did you—"

"What difference does it make? I'm fine now."

"It makes a big difference," he said grimly. "I'm not leaving you in a place where 'accidents' happen. I got some most unpleasant vibes from the gate guards last night. Telephone lines cut, private investigators, something about a tree . . ."

"It was all my fault and I suffered the consequences."

"Then why don't I stick around a few days and make sure you don't suffer any more of them?"

"Because you're too damn protective. I won't have Louis hurt again."

"He should be fine by tomorrow." He frowned thoughtfully. "He's very strong, you know. One of the strongest minds I've ever run across outside the Clanad. If I hadn't had my hands so full subduing him, I would have realized you were joined to him."

Her heart lurched and the panic she had been suppressing shifted into high gear. "I wasn't joined to him. I couldn't have been. It wasn't like that at—I must have heard something downstairs and imagined—"

"You were joined," Gunner said flatly. "And it must have been a damn strong bond to have jerked you out of bed in the condition you were in. What is he to you, Mariana?"

She opened her lips to speak and then closed them again without answering. She shook her head.

"Does that mean you don't know or just won't talk about it?"

"I don't know," she whispered. "He makes me feel . . . I'm not sure."

"Then you'd better *get* sure." Gunner's lips tightened. "Because we're going to have to take some sort of action pretty damn quick."

Her gaze flew to his face. "What do you mean?"

He hesitated and then said bluntly, "Andrew says you're balanced."

Shock went through her, followed immediately

by another wave of panic. "Nonsense. I couldn't be. I'm not like the rest of you."

"Stop running away from it. Dammit, you were *joined*. Doesn't that prove something to you?"

Balanced. Nightmare. Darkness. "That was different."

"How was it different?"

"Stop asking me questions!"

"How was it different, Mariana?"

"I love him," she burst out. Her eyes widened in horror as she realized what she had said. "No!"

"I thought that might be it."

"I can't love him." But she *did* love him. How had it happened? The knowledge was as irrevocable as it was frightening. "Maybe I'll get over it."

Gunner smiled gently. "Don't look so terrified. The situation can't be that bad. Benoit was as possessive as the devil last night, so he must care something for you. If you tell him the problem, he'll probably be willing to wait for you until the reinforcement is completed."

"There *is* no problem," she said fiercely.

"Listen to me," Gunner said gravely. "Have you ever known Andrew to be wrong?"

"No, but I'm not—"

"He told me before you left the Compound that he'd started worrying about you last year, and before I came here he told me if I saw any sign at all I was to bring you home. You know what any emotional disturbance can do to someone who is balanced."

She closed her eyes for a moment as memories flooded back to her. "I know."

"Then talk to Benoit. Tell him the problem."

Her lids flew open to reveal eyes blazing with emotion. "Do you know what kind of life he's lived?" she asked fiercely. "He shouldn't have to cope with my problems. He's had enough of his own to overcome. He deserves something better. He should be happy and not have to—"

"Easy," Gunner said quietly. "Don't get upset. It's the worst possible thing for you. Serenity."

"To hell with serenity. You're *wrong* about me."

"Think about it. Andrew says this is what you've been fighting all your life. For God's sake, admit it to yourself before it's too late." Gunner's expression was lovingly sympathetic. "We love you, Mariana. Let us try to help you."

But they both knew how poor the chances were of anyone being able to help. She crossed her arms over her chest to still their trembling. "I'm not—" She swallowed. "I'm scared, Gunner."

"I won't lie and tell you that you shouldn't be afraid. In your place I'd be shaking in my shoes, but Andrew can help. He says they've made great advances lately."

"Yes." She drew a deep breath and was silent a moment. "I want you to go back to the Compound."

"Not without you."

"I'll follow you in a few days. Don't worry, I'm through running, Gunner. I just have some ends to tie up here."

"Benoit?"

She nodded jerkily. "We owe him. We've both hurt him and I have to find a way to make it right."

He swore under his breath. "Simply tell him the truth."

"I intend to tell him the truth."

"About everything?"

"Well, almost everything." She smiled sadly. "The rest won't matter. Now go home and tell Andrew I'm doing great."

"I'm not about to lie to him."

"Then tell him I'll be home soon and we'll talk about reinforcement. That should satisfy him."

"Maybe."

"Well, it will have to do." She stood up and crossed the room to kiss Gunner lightly on the cheek. "Now get out of here before Louis wakes up. It will be easier for me to make explanations if you're not around for him to bristle at."

"I'm accustomed to being bristled at." He rose to his feet. "This isn't the end of the world, Mariana. Bring him to the Compound."

She shook her head. "He deserves better," she repeated.

Gunner hesitated before turning and walking toward the door. "I'll give you a week, and you call every single night. You understand?"

"Every night—starting Monday."

"And if you notice any slippage, you hop on the next plane."

"I'll see you soon, Gunner."

"No promises?"

"We owe him," she said. "I have to make it right, no matter how long it takes."

"Please, don't wait too long," Gunner said grimly.

The door had scarcely closed behind him when Muggins glided into the room carrying a covered tray. "Settle back into bed and have your lunch now. Mr. Louis says you're to eat every bite."

"Not now, Muggins."

"Every bite." Mrs. Muggins began humming as she wheeled toward the bed. "Brain food, you know. You're a clever lass but you can't think if you're too weak."

Mariana wished she could start thinking instead of feeling. Her emotions were raw after her talk with Gunner and she was wishing desperately she had let him whisk her back to the Compound, where there was no Louis and no painful choice to make. But even at the Compound there was no real escape. Sweet heaven, she didn't want to believe Andrew's diagnosis.

"Get into bed now," Muggins said.

Mariana automatically moved toward the bed. Muggins was right—she was going to need all the strength she could muster, not only to face Louis's questions but to try to right the wrong she had done him.

"That's a good child," Muggins crooned as she settled the tray over Mariana's lap.

"I'm not a child." She felt as old as Methuselah and doubted if she would ever again be that girl who had come to Louis in the garden. In the space of a few days everything had changed. *She* had changed. Well, if Andrew was right about her, she would need maturity and strength in the months to come.

"Why did you let me sleep so long?"

Mariana glanced up from the papers on the desk in front of her to see Louis frowning at her in the doorway of the study. "You look much better."

"I should. I slept around the clock. You should have had someone wake me."

"Why? You needed the sleep. Gunner packs a lethal whammy."

"And where is your lethal godfather?"

"I sent him away."

He sat down in the visitor's chair. "I believe we're going to have to talk about this 'whammy.' I was pretty much out of it at the time, but after going back over what happened with a clear head . . ." He met her gaze. "Something was damn strange."

"Yes."

"First, how did he get through the gates? You both seem to traipse at will past my men."

"Gunner has no problem. I have to have help."

"And why doesn't Gunner have trouble?"

She leaned back in the chair, studying him. His expression was intent, his eyes narrowed, and she sensed an undercurrent of excitement. That brilliant mind of his was obviously hitting on all cylinders. "You tell me. I think you have it figured out."

"What I figured out is fairly outrageous." He shrugged. "But then what happened to me last night was *utterly* outrageous."

"So your deduction is probably true."

"Mind control?"

She nodded. "The tip of the iceberg."

"The Russians are supposed to be doing some fantastic experiments with mental powers. The Compound is in Russia?"

She shook her head. "Sedikhan. The Clanad is under the protection of Sheikh Ben Raschid."

"Clanad?"

"The Clanad is a group of refugees who escaped from an institute in Said Ababa a good many years ago and formed a community in Sedikhan. They were Garvanians who had submitted to chemical injections that caused enormous mind expansion. They became virtual prisoners of the Said Ababans after their country was invaded. The plant from which the chemical was derived was so rare it became extinct almost immediately." She paused. "It was later discovered that the chemical also produced certain side effects."

"Telepathy?"

"Yes, in varying degrees. I suppose you're wondering why we haven't come out in the open?"

"No, the general public is more wary of ESP than it is of robots. Your Clanad probably felt they could best protect themselves by staying out of sight."

"Exactly." She went on quickly, "Believe me, there's no reason for fear. We do have laws, some of them much stricter than any an outside society would formulate for us. No one is allowed to trespass on the thoughts of anyone outside of the Clanad without permission, and mind control is absolutely forbidden, except to those who are given the authority by the council."

"Such as your policeman, Gunner?"

"Yes, and my half-brother, Andrew." She met his gaze. "You believe me?"

"I'm not saying I would have believed you two days ago, but thanks to your godfather's demonstration I have no choice. It happened. I felt it." He shook his head. "Incredible."

"Most people term us bizarre." She smiled sadly. "You did yourself, if you recall. But you're taking this very well."

"I'm a gypsy. I was born believing things other people scoff at." He shrugged. "And I know what it's like to be an outlaw. You inherited these ESP powers as well?"

"No, I just got an extra dollop of intelligence."

"Isn't that unusual?"

"Sort of." She nervously picked up the pen she had set down when he had come into the study and began to turn it over and over between her fingers. "But nobody knows what to expect of half-breeds."

"Half-breeds?"

"My mother is not of the Clanad. Sometimes the bonding produces more power, sometimes less. It's a wild strain and not predictable. My half-brother, Andrew, is stronger than Gunner."

"Then you'll forgive me if I'm not dying to meet him," he said dryly. "Gunner was more than strong enough for me."

"Oh, but you'd like Andrew," she said eagerly. "Everyone does. Andrew is wonderful. Well, so is Gunner. He was only doing his job."

"And what is Andrew's job?"

"He's a healer."

"A doctor?"

"No, more . . ." She shrugged. "Perhaps we should go into that at another time. You already have enough to absorb."

"Yes, I do." His gaze met hers. "But I still need to know a few more things, on a more personal plane. Why did you come here?"

"I told you."

"Then why did you say you couldn't have a normal relationship?"

"Did I say I *couldn't*?" The turning of the pen between her fingers became more agitated. "I must have been upset. I meant I didn't *want* a normal relationship. I like being on my own. I don't want ties or a man who would interfere with my work. I thought it would be much more intelligent to . . ."

"You're going to wear through the casing on that pen. Why don't you put it down and just tell me the truth."

Her hand tightened spasmodically on the pen, and then she carefully set it down on the blotter and folded her hands on the desk. "It was the dreams."

He went still. "What?"

"I started dreaming about you."

"What . . . kind of dreams?"

"Like . . ." She felt heat sting her cheeks. "The summerhouse sometimes. At other times it was worse. I kept looking for you, but I couldn't find you. I kept looking—"

"Searching but not finding," he murmured.

"It was *crazy*. I couldn't even remember seeing a picture of you and yet there you were in my dreams." She added quickly, "Of course, I must have seen a photograph of you somewhere or other. After all, you're always on television at some trade conference or meeting."

"True."

"And I certainly saw enough pictures of you later, so that must have been—As time went on the dreams got worse." Her hands tightened their clasp. "I had them every night. Over and over. And during the day I kept thinking about them and couldn't work. My work is everything to me. I *had* to work, Louis."

"And your solution?"

"After the dreams had gone on for about four months I decided I had to do something. So I sat down and tried to analyze the reason I was having them."

"I'd be fascinated to know what you came up with."

"It wasn't logical that I'd develop a sexual fixation on a stranger."

"And we both know how logical you are."

"So I decided it was my mind's way of signaling to my body that I needed—"

"A baby."

She nodded jerkily. "I love babies. I was lonely. It seemed the only reasonable answer."

"It didn't occur to you that your solution was a little simplistic?"

"No." She could feel the tears sting her eyes as she raised her gaze to meet his. "I had to stop the dreams."

"I see."

"I never meant to hurt you. I thought if I let you have Muggins . . ."

He was silent, looking at her.

"Pretty stupid, huh?"

"Not stupid." His voice was very gentle. "Just very, very young, *ma petite*."

"Don't be kind to me. I don't deserve it. I fouled up everything. I hurt you."

"And I hurt you. It would seem we're even."

"No, we're not. It was all my—"

"Hush." He stood up and came around the desk. "*Doucement.* It's all right."

"It's not all right." She drew a deep, shaky breath. "And I do wish you'd stop being nice to me."

A faint smile touched his lips as he leaned against the edge of the desk. "I'll watch it in the future. Would you prefer I beat you or only cast you into the dungeon?"

"It's not funny."

"And it's no tragedy. We can work this out, Mariana."

"I know we can." She straightened her shoulders and gestured to the papers in front of her. "I've been thinking about it. I've changed and initialed the contracts to give you fifty percent of the gross and full control of the—What are you laughing at?"

"You." A smile lingered on his lips. "Are we back to Muggins?"

"What else can I give you? It's the most valuable thing I own."

"You're wrong." A brilliant smile lit his face. "You forget you're carrying my child."

She couldn't look away from him. He showed no cynicism or bitterness, just warmth and glowing tenderness. "I couldn't give up my baby."

"No?" He brushed back the unruly curls at her temple with a gossamer-light touch. "You look scarcely more than a child yourself."

"I'll be a very good mother," she said earnestly. "I probably seem thoughtless and impulsive but I'm—"

"Scarcely 'thoughtless.'" He wound a curl on his index finger. "We came together because you put too *much* thought into this. I learned a long time ago instinct can often be a better guide than cold analysis."

"You're not cold."

"Many people would not agree with you."

"You're very generous and giving with your friends."

He smiled. "And I would be equally generous and giving to my child."

"You like children?"

"Very much. Childhood has always seemed a magical, mysterious time to me." A flicker of wistfulness crossed his face. He shrugged. "But then that which we've never had always seems more exotic and desirable."

And he had been robbed of his own childhood, in the cruelest way possible. She suddenly wanted to reach out and comfort him, cuddle him, as she had done last night when he was in pain.

"You're willing to share your Muggins." His tone was coaxing as he gently pulled on the curl. "Would it be so much harder to share our baby?"

"Impossible."

"Nothing is impossible." He grimaced. "As you've given me ample evidence in the last few days. Stay here and—"

"I can't stay here. I have to go home to Sedikhan."

"Why?"

She searched wildly for an answer he would accept, but only came up with, "My laboratory is there."

"I'll build you one here. Better still, I'll build you one at my place in Connecticut. I spend more time there and I'd rather have the two of you nearby."

"I'd rather go back to Sedikhan. I'm not used to being away from the Compound. I've never left home before this trip."

"Not even to go to school?"

"We have fine teachers in Sedikhan." Her tone became defensive. "And there was no reason for me to leave. The Compound is beautiful and we have no crime or—"

"Stop arguing with me. I know nothing about your Sedikhan. It sounds like a very nice place. I just found it curious you were content to stay safe at home. Most youngsters are eager to brave the world and try their wings."

"'Safe,'" she repeated. Her belligerence vanished as quickly as it had come; she realized she again was justifying the walls she had built to hide behind, telling him and herself lies to cover her fear. "Yes, safety has always been important to me," she said wearily.

"I can keep you safe." His voice was velvet persuasion, his light eyes intent, glowing. "Trust me. I would take great care of you and the child, Mariana."

"Would you?" Safety. Care. Trust. His words were weaving a spell about her that seemed impossible to break. She finally managed to tear her gaze away from him. "Lately, I've realized it's not always good to hide away because we're afraid. It's better to face the unpleasantness and accept what comes."

"A very sensible attitude, but not at all to my

liking. I'll have to change your mind once we reach Connecticut. I want your life to be all happiness and serenity."

Serenity. A chill went through her as she remembered Gunner had used that very word to caution her. "I'm not going to Connecticut."

"I'll have to change your mind about that too." He lifted her chin on the arc of his fingers and looked gravely down into her face. "And I *will* change your mind, Mariana. I can accept the fact that I have to compromise, but this time I must have something." His next words were halting. "I thought we might . . . marry."

She looked at him, startled. "Marry?"

"Perhaps not right away. I'm perfectly willing to give you time to become accustomed to the idea."

"Why?"

He was silent a moment, and when he answered, it came awkwardly. "I, too, have been lonely. I've never had anyone of my own. What harm would it do to let me build you a beautiful playground where you and the child would be safe and I could come and visit you? You needn't worry that I would trouble you in any way. I would never put you at risk as I did in the summerhouse. I just want to watch over and help you. Is that too much to ask?"

It was much too little. She swallowed to ease the tightness in her throat. "No, but I can't do it. And I can't promise to share the child. I want something before I—" She stopped and smiled with an effort. "But who knows what will happen? Someday maybe I'll send for you to come and take us to this Connecticut."

He shook his head. "'Maybe' is too indefinite."

She pulled away from him and stood up. "It will have to do. I'm going for a walk in the garden. Will you have someone go to the village and call your attorneys to tell them to be here tomorrow? I'd like to get Muggins, Inc. finalized as soon as possible. As I said, fifty percent of the gross and full authority over—"

"I don't give a damn about Muggins." His voice was suddenly fierce. "Haven't you been listening to anything I've said? It's not enough."

"I know it isn't." As she reached the French doors she glanced back over her shoulder to gaze at him with moistly glittering eyes. "But I can't do what you want. You'll have to take Muggins until I figure out what else I can give you."

Not waiting for an answer, she quickly walked out onto the terrace.

Sweet heavens, she was hurting. It wasn't fair, dammit. She didn't want to leave Louis just when she had found him. She didn't want to go home and face what was waiting for her there. She felt raw with pain. . . .

Her pain, *her* hurt, she thought in self-disgust. It was time she quit wallowing in self-pity and thought about Louis. Not only did she have reparations to make, but she had to ensure Louis didn't suffer because she refused to share their child.

She strolled down the path, her brow knitted in thought, as she considered the possibilities and analyzed the situation.

Six

"You're very quiet."

Louis leaned back in his chair and gazed at her quizzically across the dining room table.

"I'm thinking."

His brows lifted in mock horror. "Should I be worried?"

"Of course not." She took a sip of wine. "There's nothing for you to be apprehensive about. I want only what's best for you."

"How comforting. As you define what's best?"

"We all have our own viewpoints and definitions. Did you call your lawyers?"

"Yes, they'll be on our doorstep at eight sharp tomorrow morning."

"And you'll take the fifty percent?"

"Oh yes, I've decided it'll be a very good thing for us to be equal partners. As you say, we all have our own viewpoints, and I'm sure we won't be in agreement on many things. That will mean you'll have to stay close at hand to argue with me."

"Don't count on it." She looked down into the wine in her glass. "Perhaps I'll trust your judgment and leave the decisions to you. I may be busy for the next few months."

"Doing what?"

She shrugged. "Oh, this and that. I have Mrs. Muggins's programming to correct and I'm developing a Mr. Muggins for gardening and chauffeuring tasks and there are several other projects on my drawing board."

"I don't buy it," he said flatly. "You care about Muggins. You wouldn't risk having the project not carried out to your satisfaction. You'd want to be right on the spot, dipping your fingers into every aspect of the operation."

"You've only known me a few days and you can't be certain what I'd do or not do. We're practically strangers."

"Strangers, hell." His gaze met hers across the table. "We rocketed past that point a century or so ago. Stop trying to put barriers between us. I *know* you."

And she knew him, she thought wistfully. She knew his tenderness, his anger, and his passion. She knew his rigid self-discipline and his keen intelligence. Most of all she knew how difficult an opponent he would prove to be in a battle.

As she knew she was going to have to fight him.

The decision and solution she had been trying to reach all day suddenly sprang to mind full-blown as she stared at him.

He frowned. "I don't like the way you're looking at me."

"I don't know what you mean."

"You're studying me as if I were a blueprint of one of your robots whose specifications aren't up to standard."

She smiled brilliantly. "Your specifications are way above standard, Louis." She finished her wine in one swallow and tossed her napkin on the table. "I've had enough to eat. I think I'll go to my room."

"You can't run away forever, Mariana."

That was what Gunner and Andrew had told her, she thought sadly. "I'm through running. I'm just retreating to regroup my forces." She stood up. "I'll see you later, Louis."

When Louis opened the door of his bedroom four hours later the first thing he noticed was the light burning on the nightstand. The second thing he saw was Mariana lying in his bed, bare golden shoulders rising above the sheet she clutched to her breasts.

A surge of mindless lust tore through him as he stood looking at her. Mindless? But he was not a mindless animal, he reminded himself desperately. He had discipline and control. "I presume you have some reason for being here?"

She nodded. "I told you I'd see you later."

"I hardly thought it would be under these particular circumstances."

She smiled tremulously. "I decided I should check out your specifications."

He started toward her. "I'm not in any condition to find this amusing."

Her gaze wandered to his lower body. "I can see that. It's a great relief to me. I wasn't sure you still wanted me. You've been treating me like a cross between an aging invalid and a young orphan you wanted to adopt."

"You know that's the only way I can treat you to keep you safe."

"I don't know that." Her hand closed nervously on the sheet. "And you don't either. I think it's time we found out."

"What's wrong?" he asked caustically. "Did you find out our time in the summerhouse didn't have the effect you schemed for?"

She met his gaze. "What would you say if I told you it hadn't? That I'd made a mistake and there's no child."

He could see the rapid pulse in the hollow of her throat that always betrayed her nervousness, and he felt a sudden surge of tenderness. "I would grieve for you," he said gently. "And *with* you, *ma petite*."

"I'm not your little girl and I'm not a child you can designate to the playground. I'm a woman."

His gaze went to the cleavage edged by the sheet. "At the moment I have no need of verbal reminders."

He was growing more aroused every minute. He knew he had to put an end to this scene. "I'm sorry your hopes have come to nothing, but I can't oblige you."

"Why not? I don't see why—" She stopped, then sighed. "Blast it, I'm not going to tell you any more lies, even for your own good. It wasn't a mistake. As far as I know I'm still pregnant."

He tensed. "Then why are you here?"

"Because it can't go on," she said simply. "You're a very loving man who has a lot to give. You should have a wife and children and not be bed-hopping with cold, mercenary bitches who only want your money."

"And you're going to save me from that fate?"

She nodded earnestly. "Don't you see? You were a boy when Schuler diagnosed your problem. You're grown-up now, you've learned to deal with—"

"I haven't learned to deal with it, dammit."

"You don't know that. You'll never know unless you try." Her face lit with eagerness as she leaned forward. "Let's try, Louis."

The sheet had slipped until it barely covered her nipples, and he couldn't take his gaze from the outline of the shadowy tips. He moistened his dry lips. "You don't know what you're doing."

"Of course I do. I've thought it all out very thoroughly. You need this. You've told me you like me and respect me. You even feel protective toward me. I'm the perfect guinea pig."

He laughed incredulously. "My God, you're impossible. Don't you understand? I'll *hurt* you."

"I don't think you will. I'm willing to take the chance."

"Why?"

"What difference does it make?"

"It makes a hell of a lot of difference."

Her brown eyes were glistening in the lamplight. "I've taken too much from you," she whispered. "It's time I paid something back."

It was the answer he had expected, but it didn't stop the pain from jolting through him. "So you decided to seduce me and save me from myself. Then you'll go dancing back to Sedikhan with a clear conscience. Is that how it's supposed to work?"

"I want you to be happy. You deserve to be happy."

"But not with you?"

She glanced away from him. "No, not with me."

"This conversation is getting us nowhere. I believe you'd better go back to your own room."

"You'll have to throw me out."

"That can be arranged." He strode toward the bed. "I've no desire to accept charity, Mariana. It's a complete turnoff."

"You're not finding it—" She broke off as his hand fell on her bare shoulder. The muscles went rigid beneath his palm. "It's strange, isn't it? I don't feel this when anyone else touches me. Is it like that with you too?"

Her skin felt like satin, and yet he could feel the heat below the smooth flesh. Her scent was faintly floral with a touch of citrus, drifting to him in a cloud more intoxicating than opium because it was distinctly Mariana's scent. He tried to breathe shallowly so that he wouldn't smell it, but his heart was beating so fast he was forced to take deep breaths. She was beginning to tremble beneath his palm. Hunter. Prey. Lust. The muscles of his stomach clenched painfully. "No," he said hoarsely. "It has no effect on me."

"Oh." She reached up and moved his hand to cover her breast. "Do you feel anything yet?"

His teeth sank into his lower lip to keep back a groan. It was torture looking down at his hand on her breast and forcing himself not to move, not to caress. "Let . . . me go."

"I think you do feel something. Louis, just let go."

"The hell I will." He jerked his hand away, then lifted her out of the bed and onto her feet. The sheet fell to her waist and he jerked it up and roughly wrapped it around her. "Get out of here!"

She gathered the sheet more closely about her. "I didn't really expect you to give in right away, but I thought I might as well chance it." She moved toward the door. "I'm not giving up, you know. Now that I'm sure you want me I'll keep after you until you take what you want."

"Then Lord help you."

She shook her head and smiled confidently at him. "I won't need any help. You won't hurt me, Louis."

Mariana's smile disappeared as soon as the door closed behind her. She hurried down the hall, tripping over the folds of the sheet draped around her. She had known Louis would prove difficult, but she had no idea her own reaction would be so explosive.

She was trembling badly, her breasts were aching, her skin was flushed and sensitive to the touch. She wanted to go back, lie down beside him, and draw him down. . . .

She was behaving like an animal in heat, she thought guiltily. She hadn't gone to Louis for another taste of that heady pleasure he had shown her in the summerhouse, but because she genuinely wanted to help him. He had given her so much. She felt she had to leave him richer when she left him.

But surely it wasn't wicked of her to feel pleasure too. She had so little time left with him. She wanted to savor every moment, every expression, every touch.

She wanted to store up memories to light the darkness to come.

Mariana signed the last contract with a flourish and handed the pen to Louis. "Your turn."

He took the pen, hesitating for an instant before bending to scrawl his name on the four copies of the contract. He pushed the contracts across the desk toward Hendricks, who was acting as a witness, and turned to face her. "I didn't really think you'd do it, dammit."

"Why not? I told you I'd probably leave everything in your hands." She smiled at the three lawyers gathered around the desk before crossing the study to look at the landscape on the wall. "This is a van Gogh, isn't it?"

Louis followed her. "You know why not," he muttered. "You practically gave Muggins, Inc. to me outright. You didn't make one objection to the terms those legal eagles drew up."

"I trust you," she said simply. "I'll make a list of my wishes and instructions on the programming and distribution and give them to you before I go back to the Compound."

"And how do you know I'll follow them?"

"You're an honorable man."

"Honor is almost obsolete in this day and age."

"But then you're basically old-fashioned." She smiled at him. "Or you would never have thrown me out of your room last night."

"I trust you've thought better of that insanity," he said grimly.

"Did you sleep well?"

He went still. "No."

"Neither did I." Her gaze went to the golden field in the picture. "Dreams."

He stiffened.

"Aren't you going to ask me what kind of dreams?"

"No."

"Summerhouse dreams," she said softly. "You were over me and your hands were—"

"Be quiet."

"On my breasts. It was dark but I could feel your thigh against mine as you pushed slowly forward and sank—"

"Mariana!" He glanced over his shoulder at the men across the room before he turned back to her and asked in a harsh whisper, "What the devil do you think you're doing?"

"I believe I'm doing quite well." She suddenly grinned at him. "Not as good as last night, but I'm definitely making progress."

He muttered, whirled on his heel, and strode back to join the men at the desk.

She immediately turned away from the painting. "It was delightful meeting you, gentlemen. Have I signed everything necessary?" She received a chorus of assents. "Good. Then I believe I'll go find Muggins and have my breakfast." She met Louis's eyes. "Will you join me?"

"I will not," he said with great precision.

She moved toward the door. "Then perhaps I'll join you later. . . ."

"I've been looking for you." Mariana sat down on the bench beside Louis and sighed contentedly. "What a beautiful morning. The sky is so blue it hurts your eyes, doesn't it?"

"Yes." His tone was clipped. "Go away, Mariana."

She shook her head. "I've decided that propinquity is very important. It will intensify and accelerate the effect." She smiled cheerfully. "So from now on I'll be trailing behind you like a friendly puppy."

"Too friendly. And for Lord's sake, button your blouse."

She glanced down at the white tailored blouse she had unbuttoned to reveal a hint of the upper rise of her breasts. "I don't think that would be a good idea. I don't own any sexy clothes except the gown I wore the first night, but you did mention one time that you liked my skin. I decided it would be intelligent to display more of it."

"Nothing about what you're doing is intelligent. It's reckless as hell."

"Relax. I'm not feeling aggressive at the moment. I'd just like to sit here with you and be quiet."

"Quiet? You?" He shook his head skeptically. "You're too restless to sit still more than two minutes at a time."

"Well, I'm changing my ways. I've spent years charging around in a fever trying to do everything I wanted to get done. Now I'm stopping to smell the roses." She suddenly chuckled as she glanced around the garden. "And I've certainly picked the right place for it, haven't I?"

He turned to look at her. "What was the hurry?"

"What?"

"You said you were in a fever."

"Oh!" She looked down at her hands. "There didn't seem to be enough time."

"A strange attitude for a youngster to have."

"Is it? But then, I've always known nothing lasts forever."

"Nothing?" He smiled gently. "You're wrong, *ma petite*. Perhaps not material things but, if one works at it, friendship can have great staying power."

"Oh, dear." She sighed. "I'm losing ground. You called me *ma petite*, youngster, and expanded on the joys of friendship, all in the space of a minute. I guess it's time I stopped smelling the roses." She reached out and placed her hand on his forearm. She felt the muscles tense beneath her palm as she began rubbing slowly back and forth. "I'm really glad you didn't give in last night. Being in your bedroom bothered me."

He stared warily down at her hand on his arm. "I would never have guessed it."

"Because I once told you I was aggressive?" She shook her head. "Only about my work. I don't know anything about seduction, and most of the time I feel very scared and unsure of myself."

"Then forget about it."

"I can't stop just because it frightens me. Some things are worth a little emotional turmoil. Now, to get back to why your bedroom bothered me. It was because of the women." Her index finger moved with teasing lightness over the pulse point at his wrist and she felt a gratifying jump in acceleration. "I knew you'd probably made love to hundreds of women in that bed."

"Hardly hundreds. I've only had the chateau three years," he said hoarsely. "Take . . . your hand away."

"Very well." She shifted her hand to his abdomen. He inhaled sharply. "I like it better here anyway. You have a superb muscular structure, clean, well-knit, yet powerful. I've often thought about duplicating that look in a robot. But it would probably appear too menacing."

"It is menacing," he said through his teeth. "Stop—touching me."

"As I was saying, I found the thought of you with another woman very disturbing. I never considered myself particularly possessive and I'm sure it's not a civilized attitude, but . . ." Her hand shifted from his abdomen to his lower belly.

A shudder went through him; his muscles tightened beneath her palm as if galvanized by electricity.

"How do you feel about it?"

His breath was laboring. "How do I feel about what?"

"Me with another man. Is it just me? Or would you object if I did this to another man?"

"Don't talk about it."

"I think I have to; it seems to have a decided

physical effect. It must have something to do with protecting the lair and the family unit."

"More to do with the preservation of the species," he said thickly. "Trust you to analyze the response and come up with the wrong answer."

"Most of the time I come up with the right answer. I've just been striking out with you."

"And you're striking out again. You don't know when you're well off."

"To get back to me with another man . . ."

"I told you *not* to talk about it."

Her hand fell from his belly to his thigh. "I've been thinking, and I believe all your fine plans to build me a beautiful playground in Connecticut really boil down to your wanting to put me in prison."

"I wanted to keep you safe."

"Consciously, but subconsciously didn't you realize I was a responsive woman? Don't you want to contain those responses?"

"That makes me a dog in the manger."

"No, just a very human male with the usual barbaric impulses." Her hand slid around to his inner thigh. "I read a book once titled *The Naked Ape* that described—"

"No!" His hand clamped down on her wrist, holding it in place.

"Would you mind not holding me quite so tightly?"

"It's the barbarian in me." His face was flushed and his eyes glittered as he glared down at her. "And you'd better get used to it if you're going to continue in this vein."

"I have every intention of continuing what I've

started." She smiled at him. "And you notice you immediately loosened your grip when you realized you were hurting me. That means you're more in control than you think you are."

"Because I still have a fragment of sense left." He released her wrist and jumped to his feet. "Lord knows how I can manage to when you—" He broke off and strode away from her toward the chateau.

She watched him until he disappeared through the French doors, wondering if she should follow him and try to consolidate the gains she had made. No, it would probably be better to leave him alone for a while now that his resistance was once again firmly in place. She would go to her room and work on the adjustments she intended to make in Mrs. Muggins's programming. She wanted all the most urgent work wrapped up before she returned to the Compound. She shivered as she felt the familiar ripple of panic grip her, then firmly dismissed it. She wouldn't think about the Compound and she wouldn't go back to the chateau and work on Muggins.

Not just yet.

She lifted her face and let the sun bathe her in its warm, golden glow.

Right now, she would sit here and think about Louis and smell the roses.

"You didn't come to dinner." Mariana stood in the doorway and smiled at Louis across the study. "I tolerated you missing lunch, but not dinner, and Muggins was about to come after you and drag you into the dining room. Who's hiding now?"

"Me," he said flatly. "I can't take much more of this."

"That's what I'm hoping." She shut the door and came toward him, staring curiously at the heap of papers almost covering the surface of the enormous desk. "What are you doing?"

"Working."

"You came to Darceaubeau to rest."

"And then you popped into my life. Muggins, Inc. is going to take a hell of a lot of work before it's ready to roll."

She came around the desk and sat on the padded arm of his executive chair. "There's time for that later." She reached out and ran her fingers along the coarse, thick hair at his nape. "Stop and smell the roses."

"Stop—touching me."

"Why? You like it. I like it. I can't see why—"

She was suddenly lying on her back on top of the desk, with Louis standing over her.

He had moved with such lightning force and speed she could only look at him in astonishment.

He parted her thighs, his palm cupping her womanhood. She could feel the warmth of his hand through the layers of denim and cotton. "Is this what you want?" Then his hand was gone and he bent closer and rubbed slowly back and forth, letting her feel his heavy arousal. She bit her lower lip as a tingling ripple of desire went through her. "Do you want me to tell you how much I hurt, how much I want you?" His hands covered her breasts as his hips moved, rotated against her. "Do you want me to tell you how long I lied awake in bed last night fighting it, thinking about all the things I'd like to do to you?"

She gazed up at him in helpless fascination. He was exuding a sensual need so powerful it was almost tangible. She said breathlessly, "I believe it would be more sensible to show me."

"Sensible?" He laughed desperately. "I can't even grasp the concept. All I can think about is—" He closed his eyes, obviously fighting for control. Then he flung himself away from her and back into the executive chair. "Get up."

She struggled to a sitting position on the desk. She was shaking, but still managed to smile. "That . . . was a surprise. I didn't think I was so close."

He leaned his head on his hand and covered his eyes. "In another minute I would have shown you 'close.' Listen, what can I do to convince you that you're making a mistake?"

"Nothing. You can't."

"Do you know why I first went to Schuler?" His voice was so low it was barely audible. "There was a girl. A tiny, big-eyed girl . . . DiDi was like me, one of the gypsies in Gino's pack. Life hadn't been kind to her and she always seemed terribly alone. Even more alone than the rest of us. I wanted to be kind to her when we made love. I liked her; she was my friend." He took his hand away, and his eyes were bleak. "But I wasn't kind to her. Afterward, she had bruises . . . She cried. *Merde*, she was even frightened of me. She said I hadn't known who she was." He swallowed. "I felt sick. I never want to feel like that again."

Tenderness surged through her. "This DiDi

sounds like a wounded bird. She probably would have reacted that way to any man. I promise it won't be like that with me."

"You can't know . . . Dammit, I almost raped you on that desk a minute ago."

"Louis, you can't rape a willing woman," she said in exasperation.

His face twisted in torment. "It's got to stop. I don't know how much longer I can keep from—It's dangerous."

Poor Louis. Her exasperation vanished and the tenderness she felt now was almost maternal. She stood up and leaned forward to press an affectionate kiss on his temple. "I'll stop—for now." She moved toward the door. "But it's only a postponement. Good night, Louis."

Seven

"A note for you, Miss Mariana." Muggins glided forward and placed a folded slip of paper beside her plate. "Mr. Benoit left it for you before he left."

She stiffened. "Left?"

"At six forty-two this morning."

She supposed she should have expected this development after last night.

Only two curt lines had been scrawled on the paper.

> *I'll be in touch. Get over this, dammit.*
> *Louis*

She frowned as she automatically refolded the note.

"He didn't say where he was going?"

"No." Muggins started for the doorway. "And he didn't eat his breakfast. The man never eats his breakfast. I keep telling him but he pays no mind to me . . ."

Mariana tuned her out and tried to concentrate. Louis obviously wanted to put distance between them until he could rebuild his defenses against her. She must not let him do it. Therefore she must track him down and complete the task she had set herself.

Easy to say, she thought, but how was she to track down a man who didn't want to be found? He had undoubtedly told his office not to reveal his destination to her.

There seemed to be only one solution to the quandary.

She jumped to her feet, picked up the receiver of the phone on the sideboard, and quickly dialed a number.

The phone rang three times before Gunner picked up.

"I have a problem."

"Slippage?" He muttered a curse. "My Lord, Mariana, I told you that you should come back with—"

"I'm fine," she said, cutting into the tirade. "It's not me. Louis has left the chateau and I need to know where he's gone."

"Why didn't you ask him?"

"I couldn't. The situation is . . . difficult."

"That's all you need. A difficult situation to cope with."

"I told you I was fine," she said impatiently. "I can handle it."

"Handle what?"

"Gunner, are you going to help me or not? Louis

is too responsible an executive not to have told someone where to contact him."

"But they won't tell you?"

"No."

"I can't convince you to come home?"

"Not yet."

He sighed. "Okay. I'll send a man to scout around the Paris office."

"I need the information right away."

"You'll get it."

He hung up the phone.

Gunner called back at seven-thirty that evening. "He's gone to Canada. He owns a lumber company based in the Laurentians and has a lodge on a mountaintop in Quebec province called Pinehaven."

"Give me the location." She reached for the pen on the table beside her and quickly wrote down the directions. "Thanks, Gunner, I appreciate it."

"Andrew's not going to thank me. The lodge is almost inaccessible. You'll have to hike a mile over a rough path after you leave the road." He paused. "And no telephone. How are you going to contact us if you need us?"

"I'm not going to need you."

"Have you told Louis?"

She hesitated. "No."

"Great. He won't know who to get in touch with if—"

"There are no ifs. I told you, I'm feeling great, just great. Good-bye, Gunner."

She quickly returned the receiver to the cradle before he could resume his arguments.

"I can't take you any farther. I'm late getting back to the camp now." The young lumberjack stopped the jeep at the side of the road but kept the engine running as he gestured to the overgrown path to his left. "That will take you the rest of the way to Pinehaven." He frowned. "It's going to be dark in about forty minutes and you don't want to lose your way. You'd better hurry."

"I will." Mariana tightened the straps of her knapsack, jumped out of the jeep, and waved. "Thanks for the lift."

He continued to gaze at her uneasily. "I don't like leaving you here this way. You're sure Mr. Benoit's expecting you? I hadn't even heard that he'd come back."

"Oh yes, he's expecting me." She jammed her hands in the pockets of her plaid mackinaw and set off down the path. The wind whistled mournfully through the mountains, and she shivered. Pinehaven was probably peaceful and inviting in the summer but fall had already come and gone this far north. The sun was low and would soon be setting and shadows were beginning to fall over the wilderness landscape. Soon it would be dark. . . .

She quickened her pace until she was almost running.

She was breathless by the time she saw the lodge across the clearing. Lights beamed cozily from the windows, and she felt almost weak with relief. It was only a small structure, an A-frame, built of redwood and glass, with a deck that completely surrounded the house.

She trotted across the clearing, trying not to look either to the right or left, where darkness had already devoured the woods and was now creeping across the glade.

She reached the steps, took them two at a time, dashed across the deck, and opened the front door.

Louis was sitting in a chair before a stone fireplace across the room, his back to the door. The red crewneck sweater he wore made his sable hair appear even blacker in contrast.

He was staring moodily down into the depths of the blaze and didn't turn around. "You're letting in the cold. Close the door and come over to the fire."

She stiffened and stood still. Such tension vibrated in his voice that, for an instant, she was more afraid of him than of the darkness waiting outside. She drew a deep breath and closed the door. "You were expecting me?"

He still didn't look at her. "I hoped you wouldn't come." He paused. "But I expected you."

She moved quickly across the room, stood on the hearth, stripped off her gloves, and held out her hands to the fire. "Then you shouldn't have put both of us to all this trouble. We'd have been much more comfortable at the chateau." She laughed shakily. "And I wouldn't have had to run the last quarter of a mile to your lair. It was getting dark and you know how I hate"—she turned to look at him and inhaled sharply as she saw his face—"the dark."

"There are all kinds of dark." His hands gripped the arms of his chair. "You should have stuck with the devil you knew."

"I know you." She straightened her shoulders and clasped her hands behind her so he wouldn't see they were trembling. "You won't hurt me."

"Won't I?" He smiled mirthlessly. "You've made sure that I want you so badly I'm about to explode. I'm frustrated and angry and you can be sure I don't give a damn if you're afraid of me or not at the moment."

"That's good." She made herself meet his gaze. "Then it should be an excellent test run."

He gazed at her for a moment before laughing harshly. "Good God, you're incredible. This isn't one of your controlled experiments." He stood up and moved toward her. "Control is the last thing you'll get from me." He reached out and jerked down the zipper of her mackinaw with one swift movement. "Undress."

She was so nervous she blurted, "Now?"

"What did you expect?" He pulled his sweater over his head and dropped it on the floor. "You're lucky I didn't meet you on the deck. We'd never have made it inside the front door."

She unstrapped her knapsack, took off the mackinaw, and threw them both on the couch. "Will you turn your back?"

He looked at her blankly. "What?"

She began to unbutton her flannel shirt. "There's something so matter-of-fact about taking off clothes . . . it makes me feel shy."

"Shy? After two days of driving me to—" He

broke off as he saw her expression and turned his back to her. "Hurry!"

"I will." Her fingers flew on the buttons. "I know it's a little peculiar but I—"

"Nothing about you seems peculiar to me anymore." He was stripping.

"I understand you must feel that way." She took off her suede boots and her socks. "But you have to remember I'm playing this by instinct." She drew a deep breath. "I'm ready."

"*Dieu*, so am I." He turned, took two steps, and lifted her into his arms. His lips crushed down on hers, his tongue invading, toying, playing while he lifted her higher, searched, positioned. "Put your legs around my hips," he muttered. "I need . . . in."

She needed him in. She hadn't expected to want him like this, to ignite as soon as he touched her.

"Louis . . ." Her hands clasped his shoulders as she felt him nudging at the heart of her.

He sank deep and she arched back with a low cry.

In! Fullness. Heat.

His hands cupped her buttocks, holding her to him for a moment while he flexed within her.

His chest was moving in and out with his labored breathing. "Good. So . . . good." He took two steps, and suddenly her back was resting against the granite of the fireplace. The stones were rough against the smoothness of her skin, yet warm from the fire. Then she felt nothing but Louis. His hips were moving wildly, deeply, jerkily as he muttered words she couldn't understand. She clutched wildly at his shoulders as the rhythm became harder, faster. She felt possessed, devoured, absorbed. In only minutes he convulsed and cried out, holding her immobile against the stones.

She was panting. "Is it ov—?"

"Be quiet. Just be quiet. . . . It's not . . . enough." He was stirring within her, readying, and then moving again. "Help me."

She wanted to help him, but she couldn't even help herself. The passion was too hot, the need too unbearably intense to do anything but let it sweep her along.

He lifted his head. "What am I doing?" His face was flushed, dazed, as he looked down at her. "Mariana?"

"Move," she gasped. "Move, Louis. I can't . . ."

He swung her away from the fireplace and sank to his knees on the fur rug in front of the hearth.

Then she was on top of him, his hands on her hips sealing her to him as he bucked upward, thrust, bucked again.

She bit her lips to keep from screaming out with the intensity of the pleasure flowing through her. Was that her making those whimpering animal sounds deep in her throat?

Her nails dug into his shoulders as he lifted her, filling her until there was no more left to fill.

He rolled to the side and then was over her. His gray eyes glittered down at her; a tousled black curl hung over his forehead. "Again." His teeth were gritted, his face contorted as if he were in pain. "Again, *ma petite*. I have to give—"

She cried out as she climaxed and was only

vaguely conscious of Louis's spine arching with the force of his own release.

He collapsed on top of her, his breathing harsh and loud in the silent room.

Her arms encircled him protectively, lovingly. "Louis . . ."

He went still, stiffening against her. He muttered something inaudible as he moved off her and sat down on the hearth a few feet away. He drew up his knees and linked his arms around them. His breath was still labored and he was shuddering as if with a chill . . . or a fever.

He needed her. She should go to him, she thought hazily, but she was too exhausted to move.

"I told you," he said hoarsely. "You wouldn't listen to me."

"You didn't hurt me."

"The hell I didn't. I lost control. I went crazy."

"And I enjoyed every minute of it."

"You're lying to me."

"I don't lie." She struggled to a sitting position. "You didn't hurt me, blast it."

He looked at her, his expression vulnerable. "I was . . . rough."

"So was I." She grinned at him. "I bet you have more scratch marks on your shoulders than I have bruises." She crawled over and sat down beside him. "Shall we do a body check?"

He gazed at her uncertainly. "You're telling me the truth?"

"What do I have to swear on?" She held up her hand. "May Muggins, Inc. be stolen by corporate raiders if I haven't told you the gospel truth."

The faintest smile touched his lips. "How can I doubt a vow like that?"

"You can't." She got to her knees, kneeling before him, her expression earnest. "Don't you see? It's *gone*, Louis. It wasn't like that time with DiDi. You were carried away, but no more than any other man would have been. You knew who I was. You even called me *ma petite*. I've been thinking and—"

"Heaven help us."

She made a face at him. "No, I mean it. I don't know much about psychology, and Schuler may have been right about you. But I think you overreacted and would have worked out your problem in a perfectly normal fashion, given time."

"I couldn't take the chance."

"I know." She smiled lovingly at him. "Because of the kind of person you are, that would have been impossible. You could penalize yourself, but no one else."

"I penalized you." He reached out and touched her cheek with exquisite gentleness. "I didn't mean . . . I'm sorry, Mariana."

"I'm not." She turned her head and pressed her lips to his wrist. "It was like holding on to a bucking bronco. Very exhilarating."

He threw back his head and laughed with genuine mirth. "Good God, a bronco?"

Her eyes were alight with laughter. "Well, you once called yourself a stud."

He pulled her closer, his lips hovering near hers. "Would you care for another ride, *ma petite*?"

She felt the tingling start again between her thighs. "You called me *little* again."

"According to your diagnosis of my attitude toward you, that bodes well. A term of affection in the same breath as an offer of seduction."

"A very good sign."

"But I wasn't really referring to you as a child." He bore her back on the rug and parted her thighs. "You'll recall little is also a dimension. . . ."

"You see, you were almost gentle that time."

"Almost." The word was a husky growl as he burrowed his lips in the hollow of her throat. "I may never get beyond 'almost' with you. You make me feel—"

"I'm hungry," Mariana announced.

He chuckled as he raised himself on one elbow to look down at her. Firelight caught the golden glitter of the coin he wore about his neck. "You mean I'm at last going to see you eat instead of play with your food?"

"You're going to see me start gnawing on one of those logs in the basket if I don't get some food." She sat up and looked for something to put on, spotted his red sweater a few feet away, and snatched it up. "All I've had is airplane food since I left the chateau early this morning." She pulled the sweater over her head and settled it over her thighs before jumping to her feet and moving toward the kitchenette across the room. "I guess I'll have to scavenge something. Ugh. I've always hated cooking and housework. That's why I invented Muggins."

"I'll do the housework." He lazily stretched out on the rug on his stomach, resting his chin on his arms, watching her as she opened the refrigerator door. "You're a guest."

She glanced at him and then had to look quickly away. Dear heaven, he was beautiful in the firelight. Tan, hard body against soft white fur, the symmetrical line of his spine melting into tight buttocks. "An uninvited guest. Do you have enough food for two?"

"It depends on how long you intend to stay."

Casual words, but she was conscious of the sudden underlying tension in his tone. She didn't look at him as she took out a carton of eggs and some bacon. "I can stay a week."

"I see." He slowly sat up. "And what then?"

"I go back to Sedikhan and you go back to New York."

"And never the twain shall meet?"

"I didn't say that."

"Whatever. It sounded remarkably final."

"Did it?"

"You know damn well it did."

"I'm not right for you."

"You were right fifteen minutes ago."

"That was different. I'm sure on any but a physical level we'd prove incompatible."

"So I should go back to New York and find a compatible woman with whom to spend my life." He smiled bitterly. "Now that you've proved I'm safe. Debt paid, slate clean, exit Mariana."

"Not yet." She closed the refrigerator door and turned her back on him. "Another week."

"Not another week."

She broke the eggs into a bowl. "You want me to leave right away?"

"You're not going to leave at all."

"What?" She laughed shakily. "Are you going to try to keep me a prisoner like you did at the chateau?"

"No, I do learn from my mistakes." He smiled. "But just as there is more than one kind of darkness, there is also more than one kind of prison. I'm not giving you up, Mariana."

"You don't have me."

"I believe you're wrong." He cast a significant glance at the rug before the fire. "I had you there. You were *mine*."

"Sex."

"Love."

She froze in mid-motion, immobile.

His lips twisted. "Oh yes, I do love you. I've known for some time."

"Perhaps you're only grateful to me."

He shook his head. "Love. I've been without it too long not to recognize it when I run across it."

"You'll get over it." The words sounded familiar to her and she realized she had said them to Gunner concerning the way she felt about Louis. *Maybe I'll get over it.* But she hadn't gotten over it; the love had deepened, strengthened, until it filled every atom of her being.

"I have no intention of getting over it. I intend to nurture and savor it for the next half-century or so." He smiled. "And you've obligingly given me a full week to win you to my way of thinking."

"A week's not a very long time."

"In a week I learned to pick a pocket with such dexterity I became Gino's number one talent. In a week I learned how to take over a multinational company." He met her gaze across the room. "Shall I tell you what I learned in that bordello in Venice in a week?"

"No."

"Perhaps I'll show you sometime. A week can be plenty long if you use your time well." He added softly, "And I'm going to use my time very, very well."

"It won't do you any good. I can't stay with you."

"I believe you'll change your mind." He stood up and strolled toward her. "You're new at this game, *ma petite*. I have years of experience on you, and I intend to use every one of them to my advantage." He patted her fanny lightly. "Now go on upstairs and take your shower. I'll take over here. It's been a long day for you."

The complete change of pace bewildered her. In the blink of an eye he had switched from sensuality to cheerful affection.

"Okay." She moved quickly from the kitchenette to the spiral staircase leading to the loft bedroom. "You know how to cook?"

"But of course. As a very young man I worked in the kitchen of a five-star hotel, and it always seemed senseless not to pick up what skills I could from whatever job I had. I became an excellent cook." As he took a frying pan from the cabinet and placed it on the burner of the stove, the tiniest smile turned up his lips. "And it only took me a week."

Eight

"Why don't you give up?" Mariana settled herself more comfortably against the pine tree. "You haven't caught anything all afternoon."

"Fishing isn't only catching fish." Louis squinted his eyes against the glare on the small mountain lake and drew back his arm. He cast his line and then sat back down on his log beside the shore. "You don't understand the philosophy."

"It quiets you?" Mariana guessed.

"That's part of it." He glanced at her. "Why don't you come over here and try it?"

"I'd rather sit here and think." But it wasn't thinking as she was accustomed to doing it; there was no frantic pressure, no drive. It was more like drifting along in a lovely state of suspended animation, floating on sunlight. Two months before she would never have believed she could spend four days without occupying herself in a fever of work. "What do gypsies believe in?"

"What?"

"You said once that gypsies are born believing things that other people don't. What things?"

"Oh, luck, magic, talismans, destiny."

"Gypsies don't have the monopoly on those beliefs."

"No, but we've had more practice." He grinned. "And we do it better."

She linked her arms around her knees. "You're the first gypsy I've ever met."

"Did you expect a red sash and a sobbing violin?"

"No, I'd done enough research to know what you were."

He raised a brow.

"Well, the basics anyway."

He shook his head. "The surface. The basic me is what you know now."

"Maybe." She gazed at him thoughtfully. "I've never seen you so relaxed. You weren't like this at Darceaubeau."

"I'm happy," he said simply. "You make me happy."

"Do I?" She wanted to make him happy, she thought passionately. She wanted everything to be sunshine for him. "That's . . . nice."

"That's . . . nice," he mimicked. "It's more than nice, Mariana. You're forcing me to believe you when you say you're not good at words."

"Is that coin you wear around your neck a talisman?"

"You're full of questions today."

"Is it?"

"Yes, I've had it as long as I can remember. When

I was a boy I used to pretend my parents placed it around my neck so that they would know me when they came to find me." He shrugged. "I refused to believe the truth."

"And what was the truth?"

"That they'd sold me to Gino and would never come for me."

Her gaze flew back to his face. "No!"

He glanced up, and when he saw her expression he shook his head. "It happened a long time ago. It doesn't hurt anymore."

But it had hurt the boy he had been.

"Stop it." He gazed at her in exasperation. "I swear, if you start to cry, I'll be forced to do something desperate."

"I'm not going to cry." She blinked rapidly. "What?"

"What would I do?"

"I've never seen you desperate. You always seem to be in control."

"I've had my moments," he said lightly. "That's why I hold on to my talisman. I figure every little bit of luck helps."

"Has it helped in the past?"

"Oh, yes. I rose from poverty and the dregs of society to quite a comfortable little niche. Of course, hope and determination help, but never underestimate the power of magic."

She couldn't tell whether he was joking or not. "You can't really believe that."

"Why not?"

"Because it's not at all sensible. I'm sure any success you've had was brought about by intelligence and hard work and the—"

"Let's see, shall we?"

She frowned at him, puzzled.

He set his fishing rod carefully on the ground. "Come here."

She got to her feet and went over to stand in front of him.

He took her hand and pulled her to her knees before him, unbuttoned his flannel shirt, and closed her hand around the coin. "Now hold tight and close your eyes."

She chuckled. "This is foolish."

"Do it."

She obediently closed her eyes.

"Now make a wish."

"Do I tell you what it is?"

"Absolutely not. It's your wish."

She could hear the chirping of birds and the light, rhythmic sound of his breathing. The breeze carried the scent of pine and lemony after-shave to her nostrils and his skin was warm beneath her fingers and so was the coin in her palm. Sweet heaven, she wished this moment could go on forever, that she would never have to leave him.

"Did you make a wish?"

She kept her voice carefully even. "Of course not. This is all nonsense."

"Do it for me." His tone was coaxing.

"Oh, all right." There was no need to make another wish when there was only one thing she wanted. "It's done. May I open my eyes?"

"No, now you have to will it."

"Wishing's not enough?"

"*Will* it."

She was silent a moment. "Okay. Now may I open my eyes?"

"Did you will it with your whole heart?"

"With my whole heart," she said with mock solemnity.

"Then open your eyes."

She raised her lids and looked directly into his eyes. Tenderness, love, safety, enfolding her in warmth and beauty. This was the true magic.

"Now you've got to wish," she said huskily.

"I've already made my wish." His hand covered her hand holding the coin. "And it's going to come true."

"How do you know?"

"I own the talisman." His eyes were suddenly twinkling with mischief. "It goes with the territory."

She made a face at him as she released the talisman. "For a moment I actually believed you."

"Then your wish is bound to come true."

"According to Tinker Bell."

"And according to Louis Benoit." He stood up and pulled her to her feet. "Come on. The sun is going down." He reeled in his line. "If we don't start now we won't get back to the lodge before it gets dark."

She stiffened with sudden apprehension and then forced herself to relax. "I hate to spoil your fun when you're enjoying yourself so much sitting here not catching any fish," she said lightly. "We can stay a little longer."

"And then you'd be jumpy all the way home." He took her hand, balanced the rod on his shoulder, and started up the path. "Why not avoid the problem?"

"I know it's stupid of me. I'm sorry."

"Why? We all have our bogeys." He glanced at her. "But they're usually triggered by something. Have you always been afraid of the dark?"

"Not always."

"How long?"

"Since I was a child."

"A small child?"

"I was seven," she said stiltedly.

"Did something happen to—"

"I'll race you to the lodge." She broke free and started to trot up the path ahead of him. "Last one to the house fixes dinner."

"Then it will be no contest," he said dryly. "After eating your pancakes this morning you can bet I'm going to make sure I bring up the rear." Nevertheless he increased his pace. "We'll have to make the stakes higher."

"Like what?"

"Like dinner now or . . . afterward."

"I'm not sure I'd like that kind of bet. I wouldn't know what side to be on."

"Then we'll go together." He drew abreast of her and took her hand. "That way we'll both always win, *ma petite.*"

"I'll miss this place when we're back in Connecticut," Louis said as he looked down at his cards. "I think we'll have to get a chalet in the White Mountains for weekends. Would you like that?"

She stiffened. "That's up to you. Do what you like. I don't figure in it."

"But of course you do. A man's wife should always be consulted in these matters."

"Exactly."

"Of course, there are some beautiful spots in the Poconos." He chuckled. "After we're married we should really go to one of those honeymoon lodges the Poconos are famous for. I think it would amuse you. They have everything from heart-shaped beds and bathtubs to—"

"I don't want to talk about it." Mariana discarded a ten of hearts. "How many times have I told you—"

"You won't marry me tomorrow, in the future, or in the next millennium."

"Then, blast it, why do you keep assuming it's going to happen?"

He picked up the card she had discarded. "Gin." He fanned his cards on the fur rug and got to his feet. "Time for bed. Run along and take your shower while I make your hot chocolate."

"I don't want hot chocolate."

"Yes, you do." He headed for the kitchenette. "You know it always makes you sleep better. Besides, I like making it for you."

He was telling the truth. He seemed to derive genuine pleasure from performing these little cosseting services for her. The chocolate ritual was only one of many he had established during the last week, and she knew very well how dangerous those rites were becoming. When he had said there was more than one kind of prison she had assumed he was speaking in sexual terms, and certainly they spent enough time in bed. But sex was proving to be only the smallest part of Louis's campaign. He listened to her, teased her, cared for and about her. He had built the walls of his prison with exquisite tenderness. How the devil could you fight a foe so subtle and lovable?

But she had to fight him.

"I don't need anything tonight."

He smiled. "I'll make it anyway. Maybe you'll change your mind."

She stood up. "I'm not going to change my mind, dammit. I know what I want. Stop treating me as if I were dim-witted."

He looked thoughtfully back at her. "This isn't about a cup of chocolate, is it?"

"It's about you treating me like an infant." She moved toward the spiral staircase. "I have no intention of—"

"I just thought you might need the calcium."

She stopped on the second step. "What?"

"The baby. Don't they usually prescribe iron and calcium?"

She gazed at him, stunned. The bond between them had become so strong and all-absorbing these last few days that she had almost forgotten the bond that was to come. When she had thought about the child, it had been with the same dreamy unreality that had characterized their entire time together. "The baby."

He smiled gently. "We have to take care of the baby, don't we?"

"Yes." But she hadn't taken care of her child.

The knowledge exploded like a delayed time bomb. Calcium and iron pills! Dear God, she had deliberately conceived, blinding herself to her own danger and the danger to her child. Perhaps she hadn't wanted to admit even to herself the possible consequences of her condition on her baby.

"What the devil is wrong with you?" Louis was frowning at her across the room.

"Nothing," she said numbly. "I just didn't think . . . I'll drink the chocolate."

"To hell with the chocolate." He was suddenly next to her on the stairs, taking her hands. "Lord you're shaking yourself to pieces."

"I'm . . . chilly."

"You certainly are. . . . Your hands are like ice." He lifted her in his arms and carried her the rest of the way upstairs and over to the wide bed across the loft. "You must be coming down with something."

"Yes." Guilt. Sorrow. Panic.

He set her down on the edge of the bed and began undressing her. "You'll stay in bed tomorrow. If you're not better by tomorrow afternoon I'll flag down the driver of one of the lumber trucks and tell him to bring back a doctor."

She was scarcely conscious of what she was saying and was only dimly aware of Louis wrapping her in a light blanket and tucking her beneath the covers.

"Do you have a sore throat?"

"No."

A moment later he crawled naked beneath the covers and drew her into his arms.

"Upset stomach?"

"No."

He muttered something beneath his breath and

drew her closer. "Stop shaking. God, I can't stand this."

Louis was right—she had to stop shaking. This terror was the worst possible thing for her. She had to stop the panic. She had to save the baby from the dark . . .

She awoke.

Her heart was beating wildly.

She sat straight up in bed. "Louis!"

"Right here." He came up the steps to the loft two at a time. "Thank God! I was just leaving."

She stared at him in bewilderment. He was fully dressed and wearing his heavy suede jacket. "Where were you going?"

"Hike to the lumber camp to call a doctor."

Her gaze flew to the window. It was still night. "I thought we were going to wait until tomorrow."

"It is tomorrow." His expression was grim. "You scared the hell out of me. You've been out for over twenty-four hours."

Her eyes widened. "I have?"

He nodded. "Hell, I didn't know what to do. I didn't want to leave you but I couldn't wake you up."

Slippage. The first sign. Her heart lurched and then started pounding wildly. Mother of God, slippage.

"How do you feel?"

He mustn't know. But how could she hide her panic from him? "Better. Much better."

"Are you sure? You still look a little dazed."

"Fine." She tried to smile. "It must have been

some kind of twenty-four-hour virus." She threw off the covers and got to her feet. "I think I'll take a shower and wash the sleep out of my eyes. I feel like Rip Van Winkle." She moved toward the adjoining bathroom. "Poor Louis, you seem fated to take care of me. You must be sick to death of . . ." She stopped speaking as soon as the door closed behind her.

She sank back against the door, fighting the darkness as fear assaulted.

Slippage.

No, she wouldn't fall back into the pit. She was stronger than that. She would not let the fear beat her.

Block it out. Crush down the panic. Don't think about it.

She moved toward the shower stall. Think about the solution to the problem, not the problem itself.

If there was a solution.

She turned on the shower and stood beneath the warm spray.

There had to be a solution. She couldn't accept the consequences of failure.

"I made you some stew." Louis gestured to the tray on the nightstand. "After a twenty-four-hour fast I figured you'd need some nourishment."

"You're right. I'm starved." She tightened the belt of her terry-cloth robe, sat down on the side of the bed, and picked up the spoon. "Did you have some?"

He nodded. "While you were in the shower." He

was studying her anxiously. "Your color is better, but you're still trembling."

"Hunger." She started eating. "It's delicious. Strictly five-star cuisine. I think it's perfectly disgusting of you to be so blasted good at everything. Even Muggins couldn't do better."

"Thanks." His tone was abstracted as he watched her. "We're going down to Quebec tomorrow and find a doctor to give you a checkup."

"If you like." She kept her tone cheerful. "But I probably only need vitamins. It was just a virus."

"A darn strange one."

She grimaced. "But then you're always saying how peculiar I am."

He continued to frown.

She finished the stew, wiped her lips on the napkin, and set the tray on the floor. "Did you get any sleep last night?"

He shook his head. "I was worried."

"I didn't think you would." She yawned. "Well, now that you've fed me I'm ready to go back to bed. Are you coming?"

He stiffened. "You're sleepy?"

She raised her brows. "After all that snoozing I did? Not likely. I'm just tired." She had no intention of going to sleep tonight. She was too afraid to joust against the darkness without help. She smiled at him as she took off her robe and threw it on the chair by the nightstand. "Don't look so frightened. I've always been a hard sleeper, and the flu must have knocked me for a loop." She got into bed and propped two pillows up on the headboard. "Come to bed and hold me."

He stood looking at her a moment, his worried

expression gradually fading. He began to take off his clothes. "It's funny how you become accustomed to holding someone." He glanced over his shoulder and said haltingly, "It's never happened to me before."

"What hasn't?"

"I've never wanted to be this close to anyone. It's not only sex. You're comfort and heart ease and a lot of other things I've never known before." He slipped into bed beside her and took her in his arms, nestling his cheek against her bare shoulder. "It's like a gift."

"Is it?" Her throat was tight with tears as she gently brushed his forehead with her lips. "If it's a gift, I'd say it's a fair exchange."

His hand moved down to caress her belly. "This is a gift too." He nuzzled his face contentedly in the hollow of her collarbone. "So many gifts . . ."

"Yes," she said huskily.

He was an endearing weight against her. He grew heavier as he relaxed and sleep overtook him, but she drew him still closer. These moments were more precious than all the others that had gone before.

Because they were the last moments.

Mariana shrugged into her mackinaw and strapped her knapsack over her shoulders. She picked up her tennis shoes but decided not to put them on. She had to move quietly down the staircase and would wait until she was on the deck outside the lodge.

She paused to look down at Louis lying sprawled

on the bed. The blaze in the fireplace downstairs had burned low and cast only a dull red glow on the perfection of his features, yet still revealed an odd boyishness never seen while he was awake. She shouldn't stand here looking at him. Louis generally slept lightly, and even considering the sleep he had lost in the last twenty-four hours it was still dangerous to linger. He moved restlessly and she caught the glint of the golden coin on his chest.

She felt the tears sting her eyes. So much for wishing on talismans. She wanted to reach out and touch him, hold him. What if she never saw him again? Wasn't she entitled to—

She wasn't entitled to anything but to bear the responsibilities of her own impulsiveness.

She blinked back the tears, turned, and quickly and silently descended the steps.

The next minute she was out the door on the deck and putting on her tennis shoes.

The sky was beginning to pearl in the east, but darkness still hovered. She braced herself and then moved across the glade toward the path that led to the road.

Nine

Andrew was waiting for Mariana beyond the customs gate when she arrived at the airport in Marasef.

She felt a surge of relief and well-being when she caught sight of him standing there, a gentle smile on his face, his bearing exuding solidity and confidence.

His gaze searched her face. "You look tired."

"It was a long flight. Where's the car?"

"In the parking lot. I arranged for a limousine and driver to take us to the Compound. I thought we might have some talking to do and didn't want to have to cope with traffic." He glanced at the knapsack on her back. "Is that your only luggage?"

When she nodded he took her elbow and urged her out the glass doors and across the parking lot. "You scared the devil out of Gunner when you called from Quebec."

"Then we're even. He scared the devil out of me at Darceaubeau."

"He told me you wanted me to come alone to meet you." Andrew opened the passenger door of a navy-blue limousine. "I'm glad you're home, Mariana."

She settled herself in the seat. "Thanks for not saying I told you so."

He followed her into the car and buzzed the driver from behind the glass barricade. "Did you expect me to?"

"No, I know you better than that." She laced her fingers through his on the seat. "But you certainly have the right. I've been pretty stupid."

"Not stupid. Frightened." His hand tightened on hers. "There are ways we can fight it."

"What ways? Tell me what I have to do."

"Therapy for two hours every day. Perfect quiet. No emotional upsets or turmoil." He paused. "Gunner said you told him you'd already had a slippage. How long?"

"More than twenty-four hours."

"Just one?"

"I may have had another one when I suffered a concussion two weeks ago."

"If you're not sure, we won't worry about that one. How deep was the slippage?"

"Deep enough to scare me into running back here."

"Then we can't risk having it happen again. We'll set up an alarm system with the phone service that wakes you every three hours. If you don't turn off the buzzer, it will automatically ring my house."

He smiled at her. "It's not as bad as you think. I've gone through this before. I can help."

"Don't lie to me." She moistened her lips. "I know the statistics. Eighty-nine percent of those who go into balance die within a year."

"But all those who survive that year are almost always certain to recover completely. All we have to do is get you through this year."

"No, all you have to do is get me through the next eight months." Her hand tightened with desperate strength on Andrew's. "I'll do anything you say, but I have to have those months."

He gazed at her, waiting.

She laughed huskily. "You see, I've been even more stupid than you think. I'm going to have a baby."

He turned pale. "Dear God."

"I know. But I wouldn't let myself believe I'd ever go into balance. I convinced myself I was perfectly normal and it would be safe to . . ." The tears were running down her cheeks. "Even when Gunner told me it was probably true, I wouldn't let myself face how criminally foolish I had been until—"

"That's what sent you into slippage?"

"Yes, I'd only been thinking about myself and Louis." Her lips twisted. "When we're given a time limit I suppose it's human to always assume it's going to be the outer limit, isn't it? I was even dreaming about having the baby for a few months before I—" She swallowed. "I guess I was blocking out the thought that I might have endangered the baby too. Then I suddenly realized it was possible I might not have a full year and, if I didn't, I might take the baby with me." She wiped her eyes on the back of her hand. "That's not going to happen. My baby's going to live, Andrew."

He was frowning. "It's going to make your treatment . . . difficult. You probably won't be able to carry the baby to full term. Women who are going through balance almost never do. The slightest emotional upset during the last months will send you into labor."

"I won't have an upset. I'll make sure that I don't. Eight months is all I ask. Seven might do, but an eight-month premature child has a better chance."

"Mariana . . ." Andrew hesitated before saying gently, "You know bearing a child is one of the most emotional moments of a woman's life. If you go into a coma, we may have to abort the child to save your life."

"No! I'm giving instructions to the council that on no account is that to happen. You won't do that, Andrew."

"You're too damn young to—"

"I did this. No one else is going to suffer for my mistakes."

"For Lord's sake, it's your life!"

"And it's my choice."

"Mariana, you can't—" He stopped when he saw her expression. "We'll discuss it later."

"We won't discuss it at all. You know you can't go against my instructions. The council will forbid it."

He was silent a moment. "The child is Benoit's?"

"Yes."

"And doesn't he have anything to say about it?"

"No, it's my choice." She wiped her eyes again.

She wished she could stop these stupid tears. "But there's one thing you have to promise me. If I don't survive, the child goes to Louis."

"The child will be a quarter Clanad and could be better cared for here."

She shook her head. "Louis needs someone of his own. You can watch over the child from a distance, but I want them to be together. Promise me."

"We're going to do our damnedest to see that you both survive."

"That's not good enough. Promise me."

"Very well, the baby goes to Benoit."

She drew a deep breath. "Now, one more thing. Louis will probably try to follow me to the Compound. I want you to stop him."

"And how do you intend for me to accomplish that? He's reputed to be a very stubborn man."

She laughed huskily. "Oh, and he definitely deserves his reputation."

"Why not let him come? You're going to need all the support you can get in the next months. It could be better for you than a separation."

"But would it be better for him? He thinks he loves me."

"Thinks?"

"I hope he doesn't," she whispered. "He has to get over me. The baby will help but I want him to have—"

"I feel like I'm listening to a last will and testament. You're giving up before we begin."

"I'm being realistic. You told me I had to face reality, remember?"

"I remember." He grimaced. "But I didn't think

you'd do it with such a vengeance. I should have known you'd never take half-measures."

"Just keep Louis away from me. I don't want him here when I—" She stopped. "You can do it, can't you?"

"I can try. I'll call Sheikh Ben Raschid and ask him to refuse Benoit a visa to enter Sedikhan."

"Right away. We don't have much time."

"As soon as we get to the Compound."

"And I want you to send a man to Quebec to see Louis and give him a message from me."

"And the message?"

"Just have him told it's over and that he's not to try to see or talk to me."

"That's pretty blunt." Andrew paused. "And cruel."

"I have to stop him."

"Was he there when you had the slippage?"

She nodded.

"Then he's going to be pretty worried about you."

"Tell him I'm fine."

"But will he believe us?"

"Make him believe you."

Andrew shook his head. "Gunner says he's too strong."

"Then he'll have to worry . . . until he gets over me." She couldn't talk about Louis anymore. It hurt too much. "Can I work?"

"As much as you like, as long as you keep the frustration level low."

"Good. I want to finish Mr. Muggins." And heaven knew she would need to keep herself busy to keep from thinking. "I'll start as soon as we get to the Compound."

• • •

The man standing before Louis's desk was gray-ing, well dressed, and impeccably polite. Louis wanted to push his fist through his face.

"Are you quite through, Mr. Kilgrew?" he asked with careful control.

Kilgrew nodded. "That was the message from Mariana." He smiled sympathetically. "I'm sorry, Mr. Benoit."

"Then take a message back to her. It's not over and it will never be over."

"Is that all?"

"No, tell her I'll see her soon."

Kilgrew's expression was regretful. "I'm afraid that will be impossible."

"I've already been told my visa has been refused," Louis said. "It seems you people practically have the run of the damn country."

"Oh, no." Kilgrew looked faintly shocked. "We just have a very cordial relationship with the Sheikh." He turned to leave the office. "Good-bye, Mr. Benoit."

"Wait a minute."

"I really have nothing else to say."

"How is she?"

Kilgrew frowned in puzzlement. "I didn't actually see her, but I assume she's quite well."

"'Assume'? Dammit, when she left—" He stopped. The man was looking at him uncompre-hendingly. "I want to see her."

"I can't help you. Now, if you'll excuse me . . ."

"With pleasure."

Louis waited until the door closed behind Kilgrew before picking up the phone. He called

Charles Randolph at his investigative agency in New York. "I want to know everything there is to know about Sedikhan and a place called the Compound."

"What kind of information?"

"Everything. It might be a good idea to send a couple of men down there." He paused. "I may have to enter Sedikhan illegally."

Randolph gave a low whistle. "That won't be easy and would take months to set up. The Sheikh runs a very tight ship. I understand Sedikhan's borders are almost impossible to penetrate."

"Send a couple of men to prepare the way. It may not be necessary to use them. I'm pulling every string I can to get Raschid to change his mind and issue me a visa."

"That would be a hell of a lot safer."

Louis's hand tightened on the receiver. "At the moment, I don't give a damn about being safe. Just get those men in place in Sedikhan."

"We received a report from Benoit's New York company handling the Muggins, Inc. production. It's really rolling, and they should be ready to introduce the first model in six months." Gunner squatted down beside Mariana where she was kneeling, at work on the stainless-steel robot. "I feel like I'm worshiping before some avant-garde idol. Every time I come here I have to compete with one of your metal friends. One of my fondest wishes is that one day I'm going to be able to talk to you standing in the conventional position for Homo sapiens."

"Sorry," Mariana said absently, her fingers moving deftly along the complex circuitry. "I have to adjust this wiring."

"Did you hear what I said?"

"First model in six months."

"Do you want to go over the reports?"

"No, there's no need. Louis will take care of everything."

"I never thought I'd hear you say that about Mrs. Muggins."

Mariana made a final adjustment and then sat back on her heels. "There, that should do it."

"How's our Mr. Muggins coming?"

"Good. In a week or so he should be far enough along for any competent scientist to be able to make the final refinements."

"Stop that kind of talk," Gunner said roughly. "You're the one who will finish Mr. Muggins. Andrew says you're doing fine."

"Help me up, will you?" She glanced down ruefully at her protruding abdomen. "I have a tendency to tip over these days. Was Quenby this big at seven months?"

He shook his head. "But you're much smaller than my beloved spouse." He took her arm and helped her to her feet. "Did you go back for your checkup this week?"

"Of course. Do you think I'm an idiot?" Mariana stretched to get the kinks out and then rubbed the small of her back. "I'm at the hospital on the dot at eight o'clock every Tuesday morning."

"Sorry. You just seem so absorbed with Mr. Muggins."

A luminous smile lit her face. "Nothing is as

important as Sam." She patted her stomach. "Even if I forgot, he'd remind me. Sam kicks like a pro football player these days."

"You're sure it's a boy?"

"Andrew says he is. It's nice to know. It makes him seem more like a person and less like indigestion."

Gunner chuckled. "That must be comforting."

"Oh, it is." Her smile lingered, became dreamy. "He's company when I'm working, and at night I lie in bed and talk to him. I suppose you think that's crazy."

"No, I think you're very sane. We all need someone."

"I think he's going to be a very special person, Gunner."

"I don't doubt it. He has a very special mother." His smile faded. "But Andrew told me you're resisting him. That you should be much farther along in the reinforcement."

She stiffened. "So you came to lecture me?"

"I came to ask you why and if I could help."

The tension left her and she shook her head wearily. "There's nothing you can do. I've fought against it for too long, and now it's a conditioned reflex. I try, but the minute he gets in, I back off like a scared rabbit. Believe me, I do try, Gunner."

"I know you do. Only try a little harder. When you go into labor you're going to need Andrew to help you. You know how important that is."

"Only a question of life and death." She shifted her shoulders as if shrugging off a burden. "Well, now that I've been duly warned, I have to get back to work. Come on, I'll give you one cup of coffee before I kick you out."

"I don't have time for even that. I have to go see the Sheikh in Marasef. Your Benoit is causing a hell of a lot of rumpus."

"Still?"

He nodded. "He's pulled out all the stops and is putting so much pressure on Raschid that we're having trouble persuading the Sheikh that—"

"Hold him off a little longer."

"Let him come," Gunner urged softly. "The council has a sackful of letters he's written to you through them."

"I don't want to see them."

"He's not going to give up."

"He will, in time." She grimaced. "Or time will run out. Either way, the result will be the same."

"Mariana, some of the reinforcement is working. It could be enough."

"You don't have to soothe me; I'm not going to fall apart. I've learned to face it." She wrinkled her nose. "And it only took me some seventeen years to do it."

"I'm not soothing you. It's the truth."

"The truth is that I'm not doing well with the balance but I'm in splendid physical health." Her jaw squared. "Because I've done everything to insure I stay that way. I eat like a lumberjack to increase the chances of a decent weight for Sam, I swallow pills like a vitamin addict, and I exercise every day. I may not be able to control the balance, but I can give him every physical chance."

"You won't change your mind about . . . about an abortion?"

She looked at him as if he had lost his mind.

"I didn't think so." He leaned forward and kissed her cheek. "We're all worried. We love you."

"Likewise." She patted her stomach. "And I love Sam. We're a team."

"Then there's nothing to do but see how it goes." Gunner turned toward the door. "Now I have to go and try to persuade the Sheikh that his resisting the pressure of the American Embassy is for a good cause." He added gloomily, "And I know that's not going to go very well."

She waited only until the door closed behind him before she turned back to Mr. Muggins.

Keep busy. Just do your job. Don't think about Louis.

She fell to her knees and opened the stainless-steel panel on the robot's torso. Her brow knitted in concentration as she murmured, "Okay, Sam, now let's see if we can combine those two circuits . . ."

A hand clamped over Mariana's mouth, jarring her from sleep.

"Don't be afraid. It's all right. It's only me."

Louis's voice!

Her eyes flew open.

Louis's face above her, thinner and grimmer than she remembered.

He took his hand from her mouth.

"What do you think you're doing?" she whispered.

He smiled bitterly. "What am I doing here in your

bedroom? Or what have I been doing for the last eight months?"

"You shouldn't be here, Louis." She couldn't stop looking at him. It had been so long. He was the same and yet not the same. He looked older, and the bitterness in his expression sent a sharp pang through her.

"Neither should you." He sat down on the side of the bed. "You should be at my place in Connecticut."

She shook her head. "How did you get here?"

"With a great deal of difficulty and illegal shenanigans. You gave me no choice. Why didn't you answer my letters?"

"Because I didn't read them."

"Charming."

Now she could sense the hurt as well as the bitterness in him, and it was becoming more painful with every minute. "Go away, Louis."

"Not on your life."

She almost laughed at the aptness of his words. "I don't want you here."

"Then come with me." He stood up and strode across the room. "Is that the closet?" When she didn't answer he opened the door, discovered it was a bathroom, and crossed to the other door a few yards away. "I have a helicopter waiting two miles from the Compound." He pulled a suitcase out of the closet and tossed it on the bed. "You don't have to pack much, only a few clothes and any personal mementos that are important to you. We'll get anything else you need when we reach the U.S."

"I'm not going."

"The hell you're not." His eyes suddenly blazed down at her. "You've toasted me over the fires of hell for the last eight months and I'm not going through any more. I don't know why you did this but I do know you belong to me. I know it and you know it." His gaze went to her abdomen. "And that baby belongs to me too. I won't be cheated out of either of you."

She struggled to a sitting position. "You won't be cheated out of the baby. I've made arrangements. . . ."

"Aren't you listening to me? It's you I want. It's always been you," he said thickly. "The baby's only a bonus."

She looked away from him. "Well, you can't have me."

"Yes, I can." He turned on his heel, went to the bureau, and opened the drawer. He haphazardly took out an armful of clothes, carried them back, and tossed them in the suitcase. "I already have you. I just have to get you someplace where you're not protected by bureaucrats and your Clanad so that I can convince you that what we have together is worth saving and that's—"

A shrill buzzing broke into his sentence. "What the devil is that?"

"My alarm clock." She reached over and turned off the buzzer.

"You set it for three in the morning?"

"It goes off every three hours."

"Why?"

"Medical reasons." She threw back the covers and got out of bed. "Hand me my robe."

He picked up the terry-cloth robe on the chair and tossed it to her. "What medical reasons?"

She ignored the question. "You have to leave."

"As soon as you get dressed, we'll get out of here."

She could feel the aching regret sweeping through her. "Why couldn't you have believed me? Why couldn't you have stayed away?"

"You know why."

She crossed her arms to still their trembling. Calm. She had to remain very calm and unemotional. Keep the balance. "I can't go with you. You'll have to leave now. You're upsetting me. That mustn't happen."

"I'm a little upset myself."

"You don't under—"

"Don't say it!"

She took a deep breath and then let it out very slowly. Don't think, she told herself. Don't feel the hurt she could sense inside him. But she did feel it, and the echo was growing greater every moment, vibrating through her like a great bell. "Then I'll try to make you understand. I can't go anywhere. I have to stay here until the baby is born."

"We have doctors in New York."

"They couldn't help me."

His eyes narrowed on her face. "You're ill? You don't look sick." His gaze went over her lingeringly, and suddenly his expression softened. "You look . . . beautiful."

"You must have developed poor eyesight since I saw you last. I'm almost eight months pregnant and as round as a gargantuan Easter egg."

"You're still beautiful. You . . . glow."

Dear heavens, she loved him. Sorrow soared through her in a wrenching stream. "I'm not exactly sick. It's a special problem. I can't—" She broke off, clutching at a nearby table as pain tore through her. "No!"

"What's wrong?" He was beside her in a moment, his arm supporting her. "Mariana, what—"

"The baby . . ." She closed her eyes as panic raced through her. "I think the baby's coming."

"It's not time."

"Yes it is. I knew I wouldn't carry full term. It's a week shy of eight months, but it may be enough." She gasped as another pain shot through her. "I have to call Andrew."

"The helicopter is waiting. I'll get you to the hospital in Marasef."

"No, Andrew . . ." Her knees were suddenly too weak to stand and she collapsed on the bed. The darkness of which Andrew had warned her was closing in on her. "Call Andrew."

"You said he wasn't a doctor."

"Dammit, I'm *balanced*. He's kept me alive for seven months." She added fiercely, "And he'll keep my baby alive. Call him!"

Louis hesitated, then crossed to the phone and picked up the receiver. "What's the number?"

"Just press two."

Louis pressed the button on the phone and she was vaguely conscious of the sound of his voice as she fought off the waves of darkness. She shouldn't be sitting here. It was dangerous to be inactive. Andrew had told her that when she went into labor she must walk and keep on walking.

She struggled to her feet and began weaving back and forth across the bedroom. Walk. Think of Sam. Breathe deeply. Don't panic.

Louis was beside her, his arm around her waist. "Lean on me."

Lean on me. Beautiful words. . . . "Andrew?"

"He said he'd be here with a car to take you to the hospital in ten minutes. He told me to keep you walking."

"I'm trying. . . . It's hard. . . ."

"We'll do it together." He was half-lifting, half-propelling her up and down the room. "Open your eyes. Andrew said to keep you awake at all costs."

"Yes." She fought the waves of darkness. "Have to keep awake."

"Talk to me."

"What about?"

"Anything, just talk."

"Yes." He was right; there was something that was important for her to say. Something she hadn't thought she would have a chance to tell him. "I . . . love you."

"Now you tell me." His laugh held desperation. "Not that it's not exactly what I want to hear." He pressed his lips to Mariana's temple as he turned her and started back across the room. "But I'd rather you'd picked more romantic circumstances in which to make your confession."

"Had to—last chance."

His arm tightened around her. "No way."

"So tired . . . Don't let me sleep. Baby . . ."

"We'll go downstairs and wait for your brother outside. Maybe the fresh air will help you."

"Yes."

Hallway.

Stairs.

Cool fresh air.

"Take care of Sam."

"Who the hell is Sam?"

"Baby. . . . Take care of—"

"Shut up. You're scaring the hell out of me."

Strange. She wasn't frightened at all now. Her job was almost done. Louis was here and Andrew was coming to help her. They wouldn't let anything happen to Sam.

Grass under her feet.

Walking again.

Headlights piercing the darkness down the street.

Andrew.

Ten

"Keep her awake," Andrew ordered the nurse as the orderly wheeled Mariana's stretcher down the hospital corridor. "Don't leave her for a minute, not a second."

She nodded and hurried after the stretcher.

"I want to go with her," Louis said.

"Not now. She has to be prepped and the obstetrician has to examine her. She'll be all right until the labor escalates."

Louis's gaze flew to his face. "And then?"

Andrew said quietly, "We don't dare give her anything for the pain, and there will be tremendous emotional and physical pressure. Even in normal cases there's a tendency to draw away from that kind of pain and upheaval."

"And Mariana's case isn't normal?"

Andrew shook his head.

"Why did you tell me to keep her awake?"

Andrew hesitated before saying quietly, "Because if she goes to sleep, she will never wake up."

Louis stiffened in shock. "What?"

"Did she tell you anything?"

"No. Wait. Something about being 'balanced.' What's that?"

"It was discovered that combining Clanad and non-Clanad genes often results in a child of acute telepathic sensitivity. Some half-breeds go into a period that lasts for about a year when that sensitivity is heightened to an even greater degree. It's like walking a tightrope for them."

"Which means?"

"In case of extreme emotional turmoil they're prone to go into a coma."

Louis felt the breath leave his body. "Dear God."

"If they survive the year, the sensitivity declines and they rarely have any further problem. Not all half-breeds go into balance, and we've entirely licked the problem with quarter-breeds. We haven't discovered why it passes some half-breeds by and hits others."

"I don't care about the others; I care about Mariana. What does it mean to Mariana?"

"As near as I can judge she went into balance nearly a year ago."

"A year ago? But then, according to what you say, she should be safe."

Andrew didn't answer.

"Tell me, dammit."

"I don't know," he said gently. "You see, childbirth is usually a death sentence in these cases. The withdrawal is automatic and it's difficult to fight the—"

"Then take the baby."

"She won't let us."

"Do it anyway. Don't I have anything to say about this?"

"Not here," Andrew said. "She gave instructions that the baby's to live even if she has to die."

"My God."

"She feels responsible. You see, she wouldn't let herself believe she had any special telepathic powers because she knew that meant she was also prone to go into balance."

"I need to talk to her."

"Argue with her and you'll send her spiraling."

Louis's hands clenched into fists. "I feel so damn helpless."

"Join the club," Andrew said wearily. "We've all been fighting this for almost eight months."

"Without me. Your invitation to join the club is a little late. It wasn't fair. I could have been with her, helped her."

"Mariana's choice." Andrew paused. "You shouldn't blame her. She was sure she wasn't going to make it, and wanted to spare you. I suppose I should tell you that if anything happens to Mariana, the child goes to you."

"I don't want—" He closed his eyes. "Of course I do, but not if it means losing Mariana. What are the odds?"

"It's hard to say. As I told you, we're not only fighting against the malady, but her own belief that she doesn't have a chance."

"Why in heaven does she feel that way?"

"When she was a child she had a very close friend, a little girl named Carla who was also only half Clanad. The child went into balance when she was six and collapsed one day while she and Mariana were playing together. She went into a deep coma. Mariana became hysterical when the girl died a few days later." He paused. "Mariana's never admitted it, but we think they were joined at the time."

"Dark," Louis whispered. "She's so afraid of the dark." And what greater or deeper dark could she have experienced, he thought, than with her friend in that terrible moment.

"Mariana's telepathic ability was probably only beginning to develop when Carla went into balance. After the child's death Mariana repressed it, denied it. It was her way of surviving. If she had no telepathic sensitivity then she couldn't be subject to the same fate as her friend." Andrew shook his head. "But subconsciously she always knew it was there."

"It must have been a nightmare all these years." Louis straightened his shoulders. "What do we do to keep her alive? She said you were some kind of healer. Are we talking telepathic?"

"Yes. I've been able to partially reinforce her mental barriers during the past months, but there's no surety she'll let me in during labor. The emotional level is too intense and she has a seventeen-year resistance built up. According to Gunner, you're the only one she's ever voluntarily linked totally with, and then it was only because you were in danger."

"We were linked? I felt something very strange, but . . ."

"You'd have felt the link if Gunner hadn't been keeping you occupied."

"That a delicate word for it. What if she doesn't let you in?"

"When the desire for withdrawal becomes too great, she'll go into a coma."

Fear stabbed through Louis. "We can't let that happen."

"We'll do our best to prevent it." Andrew clapped him comfortingly on the shoulder. "Our very best, Benoit."

"I want to go to her."

Andrew nodded. "It's time. Come on, we'll have to put on masks and gowns or the obstetrician won't let us near that delivery room."

"You're going to be fine, Mariana," Dr. Blevins boomed as he moved down to the end of the table, where two nurses waited. "The pains are getting closer and in just a little while this young man of yours will be seeing daylight."

She mustn't go to sleep. The baby might still need her.

But the overhead light in the delivery room was so glaring. Its brightness hurt her eyes. She would close them for just a minute. . . .

"No, Mariana."

Louis's voice. Louis's hand holding tight to hers. She opened her eyes.

Louis's pale face above her, his eyes glittering above the blue-green surgeon's mask. Behind him loomed Andrew in the same garb.

"It's all right," she whispered. "Sam's going to be all right, Louis."

"I know he is," Louis said unsteadily. "And so are you."

She shook her head. "Dark."

"No more darkness." Louis's hand tightened strongly on hers. "I'm not letting you go. You're being very selfish, you know. What would I do without you?"

"Baby . . ."

"I need more than Sam. I've been alone too long. You're cheating me."

Another pain. Closer. "No!" She instinctively drew back from it and felt herself slipping into the shadows.

"I know it hurts," Louis said. "But we have to get through it. Let me help you."

"Can't . . ."

"Yes you can. Share it." His words were coming softly, persuasively. "Give it to me."

"I don't know what you mean."

"Andrew said you were linked to me when Gunner was hurting me."

Andrew stiffened and looked quickly at Louis.

"Don't want you to . . . hurt. Ever."

"I'm hurting now. Do it."

He *was* hurting. She could feel the waves of pain and sorrow emanating from him. "I don't know how."

"Yes you do." Andrew's voice. "Link, Mariana; don't hide from it. He'll keep Sam alive."

"Help me," Louis whispered.

So much desperation and sorrow. "I'll . . . try."

Louis's eyes shimmering intently above her. A swirling. A connecting. Love. Worry. Sorrow. Even more sorrow than she had thought. It enfolded her, surrounded her.

"Sad," she whispered. "Don't be sad, Louis."

Relief.

"I won't be sad if you stay with me," Louis said huskily.

"Linked?" Andrew asked.

"I think so," Louis said. "I *feel* her."

And she felt him. Warm, lovingly relentless, holding her.

Another pain.

"Breathe," Andrew said.

She panted, her eyes shutting with effort. Louis was feeling it, too, sharing it. The pain slowly subsided.

"Now open your eyes," Louis said. "Keep looking at me and don't let go."

"Wrong to make you hurt like this."

"You'd make me hurt more if you went away."

True. She knew he was telling the truth.

"And besides, what other woman has ever had the opportunity to make her man know how she felt during childbirth?" He was picturing himself with a ridiculously swollen belly.

She found herself chuckling weakly. "Funny."

"It is, isn't it?"

Another pain.

"Push," Andrew said. "Push, Mariana."

Her nails bit into Louis's hand as she pushed and pushed again.

"Almost there," Andrew said. "Rest a minute."

Louis gasped. "Don't worry, we will."

She laughed again. "It's not so—" She broke off as her body convulsed. "Louis!"

"He's coming." Andrew stepped closer. "Push!"

"It's too late to push," she said through gritted teeth. "He's—"

"—here," Louis finished.

Contentment. Relief.

"You bet he is." Andrew grinned as the doctor turned away with the baby in his rubber-gloved hands.

"Is he alive?" Mariana asked.

An angry wail echoed to the ceiling.

"Very much alive," the doctor said. "With a world-class pair of lungs."

Alive. Well. Overpowering relief swept through her. Safe. She could rest now.

"No you can't," Louis said. "Stay awake. You're afraid of the dark, remember?"

He didn't understand that the darkness seemed almost inviting now. "Tired."

"I know," Louis whispered. "I know, *ma petite*, but you can't rest yet."

"Can't hold on."

"Yes you can." He was suddenly closer, pressing something into her hand. "Hold on to this." He brought her hand up to her breast so that she could see the object in her palm. "It's magic, remember?"

A gold coin glittering under the strong light. "Your talisman."

"Will it," Louis whispered. "Will yourself to stay with me."

"You were joking. Doesn't really work."

"It will work, if you believe it will."

"Do you?"

"I believe we were born to be together; I believe

you were meant to live to raise our son. Oh God, yes, I believe. *Will* it."

"Trying . . ."

"Not hard enough." He spoke quickly, urgently. "If you're not afraid of the darkness for yourself, what about me? I'm not going to let you leave me. You'll just have to take me with you."

"No!" She flinched away from him, but he still held her. She looked pleading at Andrew. "Help me."

"You'll have to help yourself, Mariana. Gunner told you Louis was strong. I can't break the link."

She tried frantically to withdraw, but Louis was still there.

"Stay or take me with you," Louis said hoarsely.

She was so tired, but she couldn't pull Louis down into the darkness. "I'll . . . stay."

Louis's breath came out in a burst. "Then let Andrew come in and help you. Let him come all the way in and make you stronger."

"If you say so."

Struggle. Darkness sucking her down. Then Andrew was there with Louis. Steady. Golden. Strong.

"It's going to be fine, Mariana," Andrew said. "Just relax and let me do the rest."

Louis strode into the hospital room carrying an armful of red roses. "Good morning." He handed the roses to the nurse with a dazzling smile. "Will you put these in water? I'd like to talk to my wife alone."

"I'm not supposed to leave her."

"I assure you it's okay. I intend to keep her too busy with conversation for her to drop off to sleep."

The nurse hesitated and then hurried from the room with the flowers.

Louis sat down in the chair by the bed. "*Pauvre petite*, don't they ever let you sleep?"

"At night, when Andrew is here. He's the only one who can monitor me."

"I've paid a visit to our son." A smile so beautiful it took her breath away lit his face. "You did well. He is *very* handsome. He has your eyes."

"Andrew took me to see him last night," she said eagerly. "He said he'll have to stay in the incubator for the next few days but his weight is normal." She made a face. "He should be. You should have seen all the milk shakes I drank to put weight on both of us. Did you ever see such tiny toes? It's like having a doll that . . ." Her words trailed off as she looked at him and lost track of her thought. Loving indulgence, exquisite tenderness, and proud possessiveness were all reflected in his face. She wished she had a camera to catch that expression. No, she didn't really need a photograph. She would remember this moment always.

"A doll," Louis prompted.

"Oh, that wasn't important." She looked away from him and tried to gather herself together to say what had to be said. She folded her hands tightly on her lap. "It was very kind of you to help me yesterday."

"'Kind'?" He stared at her blankly. "Kind to myself, maybe. There was no way I was going to let you go." He studied her expression. "Oh, oh, methinks I should have paid no attention to Andrew's orders to make myself scarce and let him have his therapy time with you."

"I've been thinking and—"

"I knew it." He sighed as he leaned forward and took both her hands. "Okay, let's hear it."

"I want you to go away."

"It seems I've heard that song before."

"Because you don't pay any attention to me."

"Didn't it ever occur to you that I don't need you to run my life? I'm not going to go meekly away and find a docile, sensible woman to marry. After you, she would probably bore me to death." He met her gaze. "And I'm not going to let you molder away with your robots while you play the martyr. We're going to marry and live happily ever after."

"And what if this happens again?"

"Andrew tells me that in a few months you'll be safe."

"In most cases."

"In our case."

"You can't be sure."

"I have to be sure." Louis looked down at her hands. "Because I don't think I can live without you, Mariana."

She felt a melting deep inside her. "Of course you can."

He shook his head. "Do you remember what I told you in the delivery room?"

"Yes."

"We were meant to be together." He lifted her hand and pressed his lips to her palm. "So you'll just have to live to be a very old lady."

"I shouldn't let you do—"

"You're not letting me do anything. Do you remember the dreams you had about me?"

She frowned. "What has that got to do with it?"

"I was having them, too, at the same time."

Her eyes widened. "You were?"

"Searching and not finding." He held her palm to his cheek. "Only I didn't know it was you I was searching for."

"But how could you have had those dreams? You're not Clanad."

"Two possibilities occurred to me. Either your latent telepathic powers are so strong they'd bridge oceans to project a link to me that—"

"Impossible. Not even Andrew is that strong."

"Then we're left with the explanation I prefer anyway."

"Which is?"

"Destiny," he said softly. "Two people meant to be together, coming together." He reached in his coat pocket and brought out a dark blue velvet jeweler's box. "I have a present for you."

"What is it?"

He opened the case. The coin talisman shimmered brightly against the dark blue velvet.

She searched his face. "But it belongs to you."

"It's all in the family. Our family." He took the talisman out of the box and pointed to the tiny star-shaped diamond he'd had set at the very top of the coin. "That's Sam."

She felt the tears tighten her throat as she looked down at the twinkling star. "He's beautiful. . . . It's beautiful."

He slipped the gold rope over her head. "If you ever find yourself slipping, just grab hold and remember how much we both need you." His voice became unsteady. "How we'd be lost without you."

"I'll remember." Her hand held tightly to the coin. "I shouldn't let you talk me into this, but I'm very much afraid I have." Her voice suddenly vibrated with feeling. "Oh, I do love you, Louis."

"Why do you always choose moments when I can't do anything but look at you to make your declarations?"

"I'm sorry. I've told you a hundred times I'm not good with words."

"It's difficult to louse up those particular words," he said affectionately. "They always come out right."

She smiled dreamily as her thumb ran caressingly over the tiny diamond. "You know, if I do get through this I—"

"No 'ifs.' You *are* going to get through this."

She felt a sudden soaring happiness. She was beginning to believe he could be right, that there would be no more fear of darkness. "*When* I get through this I think I'd like another baby. Maybe two or three."

He looked at her in alarm. "You mean I'm going to have to go through labor again?"

"The second birth is usually without danger in these cases."

"But I couldn't take the chance of anything going wrong. I'd have to be there with you."

"Nonsense. Women go through it alone all the time."

"You won't; we'll do it together. But let's wait awhile, for both our sakes." He bent forward, his lashes nearly veiling the mischief gleaming in his eyes as he gently kissed her cheek. "You may not need a long recovery time, but I do. What I went through in that delivery room wasn't just peculiar. It hurt like hell!"

Epilogue

"Mr. Louis says you must come at once," Mrs. Muggins said sternly. "No shilly-shallying, Miss Mariana."

"Just a minute," Mariana said as she adjusted an eye socket on the robot. "I've almost got it."

"Mr. Louis says *now*. You have to shower, dress, and leave in twenty minutes if you're to get to the reception by eight."

"Stop nagging me. I've already showered and all I have to do is—"

"It's all right, Muggins, I'll take over." Louis strolled into the workshop. "Tell Mr. Muggins to bring the car around."

Muggins glided from the room, clucking disapprovingly.

"I think you've brainwashed her," Mariana grumbled. "She obeys your every whim these days."

"How could I brainwash her when she's your

creation? You've just programmed her with excellent judgment and good sense. She knows I'm usually right." Louis stopped before the robot. "What are you doing?"

"Trying to adjust the calculator in his eyeball. That way he can judge accurate distances without—"

"Tomorrow."

"Louis, I have to get this socket right. It will only take a—"

"—minute," Louis finished. He took the tool from her hand and tossed it on the worktable in back of him. "That's what you said an hour ago. This is Mr. Muggins's big night and we have over five hundred people waiting at that reception in Manhattan, panting to be introduced to him. Should I go by myself and tell them his inventor was too busy working on Muggins, Jr. to bother with them?"

"No," she said guiltily. Louis had worked hard setting up this presentation, and she realized it was terribly selfish of her to become so absorbed in the new project that she couldn't give him the minimal cooperation he asked of her. "I'm almost ready. I promise I'll be at the front door in fifteen minutes." She turned and started toward the door.

"Slow down." Louis grabbed her arm as he reached into the pocket of his tuxedo jacket. "Another minute won't hurt. I picked up your talisman from Tiffany today."

"Thank goodness. It took them long enough." She took the necklace with a sigh of relief. "I've felt naked without it."

"Mr. Galane at Tiffany wasn't pleased with it."

She frowned. "Why not?"

"His jeweler's eye was appalled by the lack of symmetry. He said we needed another diamond star on the left side."

"Oh, did he?" A luminous smile lit her face as she looked down at the three shimmering diamond stars on the gold coin. Sam, Brad, and now a brand-new star for Kate, born two months before. "And what do you think?"

"It's up to you. You seem to enjoy your time in the nursery as much as your time in your workshop. In the past five years I've found I can get used to anything."

"That sounds very resigned." She made a face at him. "I think you're beginning to take me for granted."

He smiled as he met her gaze. "No way."

Tenderness, beauty . . . and love. More comfortable now, but always as fresh and new as in that moment she had first seen him in the garden at Darceaubeau.

Dear heaven, she was lucky.

She slipped the gold chain over her head and settled the familiar weight against her breast. The necklace was no longer a safety line, as it had been that first year after Sam was born—yet it was no less precious. It had become a symbol of her life with Louis. "We'll certainly have to take it under advisement and talk about it in a few years. Everyone knows Tiffany is an authority on these things." She smiled lovingly at him. "We just may need another star."

THE EDITOR'S CORNER

For the best in summertime reading, look no further than the six superb LOVESWEPTs coming your way. As temperatures soar, what better way is there to escape from it all than by enjoying these upcoming love stories?

Barbara Boswell's newest LOVESWEPT is guaranteed to sweep you away into the marvelous world of high romance. A hell raiser from the wrong side of the tracks, Caleb Strong is back, and no red-blooded woman can blame Cheyenne Whitney Merit for giving in to his STRONG TEMPTATION, LOVESWEPT #486. The bad boy who left town years ago has grown into one virile hunk, and his hot, hungry kisses make "good girl" Cheyenne go wild with longing. But just as Caleb burns with desire for Cheyenne, so is he consumed by the need for revenge. And only her tender, healing love can drive away the darkness that threatens their fragile bond. A dramatic, thrilling story that's sensuously charged with unlimited passion.

The hero and heroine in SIZZLE by Marcia Evanick, LOVESWEPT #487, make the most unlikely couple you'll ever meet, but as Eben James and Summer Hudson find out, differences add spice to life . . . and love. Eben keeps his feet firmly planted in the ground, so when he discovers his golden-haired neighbor believes in a legendary sea monster, he's sure the gods are playing a joke on him. But there's nothing laughable about the excitement that crackles on the air whenever their gazes meet. Throwing caution to the wind, he woos Summer, and their courtship, at once uproarious and touching, will have you believing in the sheer magic of romance.

Welcome back Joan J. Domning, who presents the stormy tale of love lost, then regained, in RAINY DAY MAN, LOVESWEPT #488. Shane Halloran was trouble with a capital *T* when Merle Pierce fell hard for him in high school, but she never believed the sexy daredevil would abandon her. She devoted herself to her teenage advice column and tried to forget the man who ruined her for others. Now, more than twenty years later, fate intervenes, and Shane learns a truth Merle would have done anything to hide from him. Tempers flare but are doused in the sea of their long-suppressed passion for each other. Rest assured that all is forgiven between these two when the happy ending comes!

With her spellbinding sensuality, well-loved author Helen Mittermeyer captures A MOMENT IN TIME, LOVESWEPT #489. Hawk Dyhart acts like the consummate hero when he bravely rushes into the ocean to save a swimmer from a shark. Never mind that the shark turns out to be a diving flag and the swimmer an astonishingly beautiful woman who's furious at being rescued. Bahira Massoud is a magnificently exotic creature that Hawk must possess, but Bahira knows too well the danger of surrendering to a master of seduction. Still, she aches to taste the desire that Hawk arouses in her, and Hawk must walk a fine line to capture this sea goddess in his arms. Stunning and breathtaking, this is a romance you can't let yourself miss.

Let Victoria Leigh tantalize you with LITTLE SECRETS, LOVESWEPT #490. Ex-spy turned successful novelist I. J. Carlson drives Cassandra Lockland mad with his mocking glances and wicked come-ons. How could she be attracted to a man who provokes her each time they meet? Carlson sees the fire beneath her cool facade and stokes it with kisses that transform the love scenes in his books into sizzling reality. Once he breaches her defenses and uncovers her hidden fears, he sets out on a glorious campaign to win her trust. Will she be brave enough to face the risk of loving again? You'll be thoroughly mesmerized by this gem of a book.

Mary Kay McComas certainly lands her hero and heroine in a comedy of errors in ASKING FOR TROUBLE, LOVESWEPT #491. It all starts when Sydney Wiesman chooses Tom Ghorman from the contestants offered by the television show *Electra-Love*. He's smart, romantic, funny—the perfect man for the perfect date—but their evening together is filled with one disaster after another. Tom courageously sees them through each time trouble intervenes, but he knows this woman of his dreams can never accept the one thing in his life he can't change. Sydney must leave the safe and boring path to find the greatest adventure of all—a future with Tom. Don't miss this delectable treat.

FANFARE presents four truly spectacular books in women's popular fiction next month. Ask your bookseller for TEXAS! CHASE, the next sizzling novel in the TEXAS! trilogy by bestselling author Sandra Brown, THE MATCHMAKER by critically acclaimed Kay Hooper, RAINBOW by the very talented Patricia Potter, and FOLLOW THE SUN by ever-popular Deborah Smith.

Enjoy the summer with perfect reading from LOVESWEPT and FANFARE!

With every good wish,

Carolyn Nichols

Carolyn Nichols
Editor
LOVESWEPT
Bantam Books
666 Fifth Avenue
New York, NY 10103

60 Minutes to a Better, More Beautiful You!

N ow it's easier than ever to awaken your sensuality, stay slim forever—even make yourself irresistible. With Bantam's bestselling subliminal audio tapes, you're only 60 minutes away from a better, more beautiful you!

__ 45004-2	**Slim Forever**	$8.95
__ 45035-2	**Stop Smoking Forever**	$8.95
__ 45022-0	**Positively Change Your Life**	$8.95
__ 45041-7	**Stress Free Forever**	$8.95
__ 45106-5	**Get a Good Night's Sleep**	$7.95
__ 45094-8	**Improve Your Concentration**	$7.95
__ 45172-3	**Develop A Perfect Memory**	$8.95

Bantam Books, Dept. LT, 414 East Golf Road, Des Plaines, IL 60016

Please send me the items I have checked above. I am enclosing $_____ (please add $2.50 to cover postage and handling). Send check or money order, no cash or C.O.D.s please. (Tape offer good in USA only.)

Mr/Ms _____

Address _____

City/State _____ Zip _____

LT-2/91

Please allow four to six weeks for delivery.
Prices and availability subject to change without notice.